Blackwing Dragon

ISBN-13: 978-1536989588
ISBN-10: 1536989584
Copyright © 2016, T. S. Joyce
First electronic publication: August 2016

T. S. Joyce
www.tsjoyce.com

All Rights Are Reserved. No part of this book may be used or reproduced in any manner whatsoever without written permission, except in the case of brief quotations embodied in critical articles and reviews. The unauthorized reproduction or distribution of this copyrighted work is illegal. No part of this book may be scanned, uploaded or distributed via the Internet or any other means, electronic or print, without the author's permission.

NOTE FROM THE AUTHOR:

This book is a work of fiction. The names, characters, places, and incidents are products of the writer's imagination or have been used fictitiously and are not to be construed as real. Any resemblance to persons, living or dead, actual events, locale or organizations is entirely coincidental. The author does not have any control over and does not assume any responsibility for third-party websites or their content.

Published in the United States of America

First digital publication: August 2016
First print publication: August 2016

Editing: Corinne DeMaagd
Cover Photography: Wander Aguiar
Cover Model: Nick Bennett

DEDICATION

For my Kansas beauties and sisters from another mister, Amy and Annika.

ACKNOWLEDGMENTS

I couldn't write these books without my amazing team behind me. A huge thanks to Corinne DeMaagd, for helping me to polish my books, and for being an amazing and supportive friend. And to my man and our two cubs, who put up with a lot of crazy work hours from me and take everything in stride. I won't turn into a total mushpot right now, but my little family inspires me and keeps me going in so many more ways than they even know.

And last but never least, thank you, awesome reader. You have done more for me and my stories than I can even explain on this teeny page. You found my books, and ran with them, and every share, review, and comment makes release days so incredibly special to me. 1010 is magic and so are you.

PROLOGUE

He couldn't do this. Kane did an about-face on the cracked sidewalk of Jeremy Jacob's house and made his way back to his car. He didn't even know why Jeremy had invited him to this party. They didn't run in the same circles at school, and the football quarterback was a black bear shifter. It would be best to stay far away from Jeremy so his heightened senses didn't pick up the monster inside of Kane.

When a heartbroken sound drifted to him on the wind, he froze, legs locked against the concrete. It was unseasonably cold in the mountains of Wyoming, and the tree branches in the surrounding woods were creaking their unease in the breeze. Maybe he'd imagined the sound.

Kane looked back over his shoulder and narrowed his eyes at the shadow that passed in front of the window. There was just one. Where was everybody? He scanned the street, but other than Jeremy's black Mustang, his car was the only one here.

He's fucking with you, The Darkness inside of him said. *You should punish him.*

Kane took an unintentional step toward Jeremy's house, clenched his hands, and forced his body to stop. The push was still there—the one that sometimes made him do things he didn't want to do. Eighteen years sharing a body with The Darkness, and he still fought for control. This was why he was a loner, why he couldn't connect with other people. Other humans. The Darkness had too much control, and Kane could never, ever let anyone know who he was. The Last Immortal Dragon would kill him if he found out about Kane's lineage.

Another soft sniffle reached him on the wind. So, he hadn't been mistaken. Jeremy forgotten, Kane strode for the woods.

There were a hundred cons to the animal inside of him, but on the only bright side, his senses were heightened. He had to fight to keep in his own skin, but he could hear, see, and smell better than humans.

When he inhaled deeply, he could smell her—the reason he'd come here in the first place. Sarah Newman had been nice to him in the classes they shared. He was a senior in high school, and she was a couple grades below. Sarah was sweet. Much too sweet for The Darkness, but Kane couldn't help being drawn to a person with so much light inside of them.

Sarah sat deep in the woods between two ferns with her back to him, her knees drawn up to her chest. Her bare skin glowed white and pale in the half-moon light. Her shoulders were shaking, and she didn't smell right. There was no scent of vanilla body spray here in the dark woods. She smelled like salty tears and pennies instead.

Something awful had happened to her.

"Sarah?" Kane asked gently.

She startled hard and skittered away from him like a frightened crab. Kane stopped, knelt down a few yards in front of her.

"Kane?" she asked in a pitiful, tear-stained voice. Her long blond hair hung limply in front of her face, but what he could see of her eyes, they looked wrong.

He forced himself not to look at her naked body. She was trying to cover herself up.

"What happened," he asked, standing and pulling his T-shirt over his head.

"Don't get too close," she whispered, averting her eyes. "I don't want to hurt you."

The Darkness inside of him practically laughed. Sarah was a buck-ten max, with the dominance of a field mouse. But as he stepped closer, Kane could feel it—something heavy lingered in the air around her. A soft snarl rattled her chest, followed by a long, keening sob.

"Look at me," he demanded, dread dumping into his system.

"Kane, it's too late to do anything."

"Look at me!"

She jerked her startled gaze to his, and the proof was there. Her eyes glowed an icy, inhuman blue.

"Fuck," he said, chest heaving.

Kill him.

"Who did this?" Kane whispered, already knowing the answer. He couldn't sic The Darkness on an innocent, though. He had to make sure.

"You know who." Sarah sounded disgusted.

"Jeremy told me there was going to be a party, but when I showed up, it was just him, and his parents weren't home. He's been asking me out, but I like you," she sobbed. "I wanted you to ask me out so I kept putting him off, waiting for you to ask me. He said you would be here tonight, and I bought a new dress." Her voice hitched, tears streaming down her face as she tumbled on. "I was going to be brave tonight and ask you if you want to go out with me, but Jeremy turned me into this...this...monster."

"Did he—"

"No," she said, the answer coming out in a rush. "He kissed me and pulled my hair, and before I knew what was happening, he bit me." She covered her face with her hands and fell apart. Streams of crimson shone in the moonlight, trickling down her arm. "I was a bear. My body ripped apart, and I was a bear. He left me out here, and I didn't know what to do or if I could turn back into...into...me!" When she dropped her hands from her face, her eyes were almost white with panic. "What am I going to tell my parents? They're anti-shifter, Kane! They will hate me. I can feel it inside of me waiting to tear out of me again." She was panting now, sucking breath desperately. "I'll have to leave school, and my friends won't want anything to do with me, and for what? I don't understand why he did this!"

Kane knelt in front of her, his T-shirt clutched in one hand. With his other, he brushed her hair aside, exposing Jeremy's deep bite mark on her shoulder.

"Why?" she asked in a trembling whisper.

Because he wants to die.

Kane winced at the anger that rocked through his body. Swallowing hard, he said, "He bit you to claim you. You're his now by shifter law. By shifter tradition."

Sarah's eyes widened in fear. She'd just been forced into a pairing, forced into a crew she knew nothing about. Her animal had been forced into her and would probably always be hard to manage. He wanted to tell her everything would be okay and that she would keep her family and friends, keep going to school like nothing had happened. But Sarah was right. Fifteen years old, and her life as she knew it was over. Jeremy had just put a long, dark shadow over the entire remainder of her existence.

A long, deep rumble vibrated from his chest.

"Your eyes," Sarah murmured in horror.

Oh, Kane knew what he looked like. Face twisted up like a beast, eyes bright green, pupils elongated. The Darkness pulsed powerfully in his chest. Sarah cowered, exposing her neck by instinct. She smelled of terror.

Kane hated everything.

He reached for her, to help her put on his shirt, but she jerked away and gasped.

"I won't hurt you." But his voice came out monstrous and deep. He sounded like the demon that dwelled inside of him.

Sarah snatched the shirt from him and scrambled up. With shaking hands, she pulled it over her head and stretched the hem down to her bare knees. "I think I need to go home now."

Kane nodded once and gestured to her bare feet. "You want me to carry you?"

Sarah was crying again, and her tears made little pit-pat sounds against the dry leaves as she looked down at her toes. She sniffed hard. "I'm fine."

Kane huffed a breath. Sarah would rather cut her feet to hell on the forest floor than let him touch her. With a nod, he led her back toward Jeremy's house. When she cried out behind him and stumbled, he couldn't do this shit anymore. He couldn't listen to her cry and whimper as twigs broke under her feet. So he turned and blurred to her, caught her before she hit the ground, and pulled her folded body tight against his chest. And without a word, he strode through the woods with the terrified, frozen girl in his arms. The girl who had been ruined for always by a boy who didn't like to be told "no."

His rage at Jeremy was infinite.

Kill him, Kane. Avenge her.

Kane gritted his teeth as The Darkness throbbed inside of him, growing more powerful with every pulse.

Sarah was panting shallowly now, as if she couldn't breathe at all. As if she was choking on his dominance. Fuck. Kane walked faster and put her down as soon as he was in Jeremy's yard. He backed away from her a few yards and ran his hand through his hair, exposed his neck. Probably wouldn't make The Darkness feel less heavy, not now that she had heightened instincts, but he didn't want to traumatize her any more than she already was.

He ruined her. Pull his head from his body and teach him a lesson. Teach him not to touch what is ours. Teach him he is nothing. Burn him. Devour his ashes.

Kane should leave with her. He should tuck her in his car and take her home and call the police, comfort her as she told the authorities exactly what Jeremy had done to her. There were laws against forced claimings. Severe ones.

Not severe enough. Ashes, ashes.

The Darkness was right. Human laws wouldn't fix the claiming mark. They wouldn't fix the crew she'd just been forced into. They wouldn't serve justice to her ruined life.

"Do you know how to drive?" he gritted out.

"I'm in driver's ed."

Good enough. Kane tossed her the keys. "My phone is in the console. Go home. Call the cops. Give them your full statement."

"What do I tell them about you?"

Confused, Kane frowned and shook his head.

Sarah whispered, "You aren't registered, Kane. And you're...you're..." *A monster.*

She didn't have to say that last part. He could see it in her blown-out, horrified pupils. He could smell it in the bitter terror that wafted from her skin. She had been mistreated by Jeremy tonight and now had a black bear scratching at her insides, but here she was focused on him. Scared of him.

She'll come around if we kill him. She's like us now. A shifter. She's tougher. We won't break her now. She could survive us.

The Darkness didn't see it. Didn't understand. Sarah being like them was a bad thing. "Tell them what you want."

"What are you going to do?"

The less she knew, the better for her. Kane shook his head and gave her a warning look.

A tiny gasp left her lips, and realization flashed through her blazing eyes. Tugging at the hem of his T-shirt, she padded toward the driver's side of his car. But before she got in, she locked her eyes bravely on Kane's. "I don't want to be his claim, or his mate, or part of his crew. I don't want any of this. Do you understand?"

Triumph pulsed through him, and gooseflesh raised all over his body, the first sign of an imminent Change. Sarah didn't know what she had just done. What she had given The Darkness permission to do. But as she fiercely held his gaze for a few seconds more, her eyes full of fury and tears, he began to think that perhaps she did. Perhaps she knew she was unleashing hell on the boy who had taken her humanity.

Sarah ground the gears backing out of the driveway, but before she left, she rolled down the window and threw something out into the yard. Kane watched her leave until the taillights faded into the night, and then he dragged his gaze to his cell phone resting on the mowed grass.

Sarah wasn't calling the cops.

She was leaving justice in his hands.

The Darkness twisted Kane's lips into a wicked smile. He turned and strode up the sidewalk, out of control of his body now, his skin humming with anticipation. He didn't knock, but kicked open the front door. It slammed against the wall, splintering at the point where the deadbolt had ripped through.

Jeremy was sitting in the living room, his boot resting on the table, a smirk on his face as though proud of what he'd done to Sarah.

"Do you like your party?"

"Why did you do this?" Kane asked.

"Because I know what you are, asshole. I know

you're unregistered. I know you have your sights on my girl, and now you can't touch her. Shifter law says."

"She didn't want the animal," Kane ground out.

"Yeah, well she thought she didn't want me either, but things will change now. Her bear will feel grateful to me. She exists because of me. Give it time, *grizzly*. She's mine now, and someday she'll thank me for what I did to her."

"Grizzly," Kane repeated, moving slowly around the couch.

"Yeah. I knew you were a shifter from the first time you came into my school. You feel big." Jeremy stood slowly to his full height. "I don't know how you hide your scent, but you're a fucking grizzly."

Rage rocked Kane, rattled him from the inside out. He had no control as his feet moved one in front of the other. *Darkness, don't kill him. Just teach him a lesson.* He had to keep his body or The Darkness would take it too far.

He bolted for Jeremy, but the asshole was ready. His fist slammed into Kane's jaw, and pain blasted through his face, but he was in it now, fully enraged, barely in control. Kane grabbed the back of his neck and head butted him in the nose with a satisfying crack. He hoped it healed crooked and Jeremy thought of him every time he looked in the fucking mirror. Jeremy shoved Kane into a table against the wall. The lamp on it shattered when they pummeled each other, punching, shoving, brawling. Jeremy snarled, his eyes the light blue he'd forced into Sarah's eyes tonight. Kane's control was slipping. It was Jeremy's bear that drew The Darkness ever closer to the surface, that challenged him, dared him. *Stay human!*

Jeremy went to the ground and grabbed a jagged glass shard from the lamp and slammed it into Kane's neck. Kane dropped, struggling for breath, but Jeremy wasn't done.

Hold on. Don't Change. Black rage was drifting through his soul like a thick fog, and Kane was losing. Losing blood, losing air, losing to Jeremy, losing to The Darkness. He pulled the glass out of his neck, and it gushed with warmth. Jeremy was on him, straddling him, hitting him, but Kane still desperately held his control because Jeremy didn't understand. He wasn't fighting a grizzly. He was going to push too far, and Kane wouldn't be able to keep him alive.

"Fuckin' grizzlies, think you own the whole goddam planet!" Jeremy screamed. He stopped hitting Kane long enough to lean down and smile in his face. His teeth dripped red. "Well you don't own Sarah. I do, *grizzly*."

"I'm not a grizzly," Kane gritted out, his limbs seizing as The Darkness took him. Kane had been shielding his eyes, trying to protect his identity so Jeremy couldn't tell everyone what he was when this was over, but now he lifted his gaze to Jeremy's and locked on.

Shock replaced the rage in Jeremy's face. "W-what are you?"

Kane was barely there anymore, just a sliver of consciousness in his head. *No, no, no! Jeremy run!*

The Darkness smiled and made two warning clicks with his Firestarter deep in his throat so Jeremy could hear the fires of hell coming for him. "I'm the last Blackwing Dragon."

And then everything went black.

ONE

"Where are you?" Rowan said low into the phone as her attention dashed this way and that through the airport terminal.

"I need to tell you something," her great grandfather, Damon, said. "You're going to stress out—"

"No, no, no," she murmured, adjusting the strap of her carry-on bag. "You aren't backing out of this. I can't do this alone!"

"You can—"

"I can't. People are staring." She couldn't pull in a deep enough breath to stop the panic freezing her lungs. "The only reason I said yes was because you swore you were coming with me."

"If I didn't tell you that, you wouldn't have gone to the airport."

"Damon, please. Please! Don't make me do this alone. I don't want to leave my mountains."

"*My* mountains," he rumbled in a deep, rattling voice. "

"Excuse me," a woman said from behind her, touching her elbow gently.

Rowan startled hard and jumped out of the way, giving the woman and her three kids a ridiculously big amount of space to pass between her and a pillar. Concern flashed in the lady's eyes as she passed, huddling her littles close. If she knew what Rowan was, she wouldn't have allowed her family even this near. And now Rowan was going to shove herself into a tiny plane like a sardine with complete strangers? Without Damon? Hell no.

"I'm coming home," she gritted out into the phone.

"The fuck you are," Damon said, his voice still too low and gravelly. "You are a Bloodrunner, Rowan. And not a small one. Your dragon is almost as big as mine, and you have the fire. Now I'm fine with you living with the Gray Backs for the rest of your life if you at least go out and see the world before you settle."

"But my treasure—"

"Is in your suitcase and will be in Asheville when you land. Rowan, there is nothing stopping you from helping the Bloodrunners."

"But—"

"But nothing. Get on that plane."

The line went dead, and Rowan glared at the screen as it faded to black. The last part had sounded an awful lot like an order. Damon wasn't her alpha, though. Creed Barnett, her father, was, and she didn't have to take orders from Damon. She could just leave and go back where she was safe and comfortable. Where her dragon felt in control.

Bloodrunner. She gritted her teeth. *Thanks for that, Damon.* His genetics had put a monster dragon in the middle of a submissive woman. His genetics had made controlling her inner monster a relentless chore from birth. His genetics had made her different from everyone. It wasn't a good thing, being a special little snowflake. All her dragon did was bring her attention she didn't want.

Rowan stared longingly at the mother and her

three kids.

She would give anything to be human.

"You dropped this." A man holding the straps of a black duffle bag over his shoulder stooped and picked a plane ticket off the floor. He stood easily enough and got taller and taller until she backed up a step just to look him in the face. He wore a black hoodie over dark hair and sunglasses, and a three-day black beard shadowed his chiseled jaw. His hair was longer on top and fell forward in front of his face. He shifted his weight to the side, and behind his sunglasses, his dark eyebrows winged up. He shook the paper gently. Right, she needed that.

She swallowed hard, took the ticket from his fingertips. There were tendrils of tattoo ink that curved out from under his sleeve and covered his hand.

"Thank you." Her words came out nothing more than a frightened croak. Some Bloodrunner Dragon she was, afraid of a human.

A handsome human with muscles pushing against the long sleeves of his hoodie and powerful legs pressing against the threadbare fabric of his worn jeans, but a human nonetheless. She'd dated one once. They broke easily.

He was staring. At least, she thought he was. All she could see was her own reflection in his sunglasses. She looked petrified. He parted his lips to say something, but a woman announced over the loudspeaker, "All military personal and veterans, you can board now."

The man turned abruptly and made his way toward the kiosk. He was the only one who walked to the front, and Rowan had to look around the broad shoulders of a man in a business suit to watch him. Tall Dark and Mysterious bore a deep limp. The woman up front took his ticket and talked just low enough that Rowan couldn't hear. He answered, but all she caught was a deep, rich tone to his voice.

So, he was military. Points for him.

Rowan drifted closer, enamored by how his arm filled out his hoodie on the shoulder he carried the duffle bag. As he limped to the open doorway to board, he turned his face and seemed to look directly at her. A small gasp left her lips, but before she could force her attention anywhere else and pretend she wasn't staring at him, Tall Dark and Mysterious was gone.

"First class and priority, you are free to board," the woman announced over the speakers.

Rowan clutched the strap of her bag and looked longingly at the hallway that would get her back to the parking garage and back to Damon's Mountains. She was twenty-five and had never flown on a plane. Why? Because the one time she'd left Saratoga, Wyoming was to aid her cousin Harper's crew a couple weeks ago. And instead of stuffing herself into a plane, she made like a smart dragon and flapped her wings instead. Which is what she should be doing now, but she was moving temporarily to Harper's Mountains on Weston Novak's relentless requests to protect shifters much more dominant than her. Made no damn sense, but okay, maybe if she spewed fire and looked tough, the vamps, ravens, and werewolves would leave them alone. If she wasn't bringing everything she could fit into four suitcases, including her treasure, she would've happily flown her own ass to North Carolina.

"Group one, you are free to board."

Eight tiny months, and Harper would have her baby and be able to shift into her dragon and protect her own crew, but so much could go wrong in that amount of time. And if anything happened to the Bloodrunners because she hadn't protected them, well…Rowan would never be able to forgive herself. No more sleeping soundly, no more easy conscience, nothing. It would wreck her.

But…there were reasons—deep, big reasons—she hadn't wanted to leave Damon's Mountains before, and taking this leap of faith that she would be all right away from home was terrifying.

"Group two, you are free to board."

Shit, that was her. That should've been the first clue that Damon wasn't coming with her. He'd been fine with flying coach. Damon Daye didn't do anything less than first class, but she was on a budget. She'd been epically duped.

Her phone vibrated in her hand, and Weston's name drifted across the caller ID. Before she could stop it, her dragon let off a soft, irritated growl. The mom with the three kids turned around and gave Rowan a wide-eyed look. Crap. It's not like she was an unregistered shifter, and the airline knew she was taking this flight, but it was best not to announce to the humans she was about to sit in a tiny plane near them for most of the day.

Rowan ignored the call because she already knew what Weston would say.

A text chirped on her phone, and she read it.

Don't be a chicken shit.
Harper needs you.

Fuckin' Novak Raven. It was his fault she'd had to leave Damon's Mountains two weeks ago. If they hadn't grown up in the same crew, she wouldn't have even considered putting herself at risk like that. And now he was making her do this. If she was completely honest with herself, she was pissed at him.

Get on the plane.

Asshole sounded like Damon now. Rowan turned off her phone.

"Last call for flight two-forty-five, last call."

When Rowan looked up, she was alone in the terminal. The woman taking tickets was staring at her, and another lady behind the counter gestured her toward the gate.

Oooh, she really didn't want to do this. What if

The Sickening started in the plane, or she had an uncontrolled Change and killed everyone in there? God, that was a morbid thought.

But...

Tall Dark and Mysterious was somewhere in that plane. That made it a fraction more appealing. She could stare at him between the seats or maybe sneak a picture and send it to Aunt Willa and they could ogle him together.

"Last call, honey," the lady behind the counter called to Rowan. "We're about to close the doors."

Harper did need her. All the Bloodrunners did. She would be shit in an actual fight, but maybe by her being there, crew enemies would stay away and let Harper grow her baby in peace.

"Miss?" the woman taking tickets called. "They're closing the doors."

Indeed, a portly man was preparing to pull it closed.

With another pissed-off rumble, Rowan strode deliberately for the gate, gave her ticket, forced herself not to turn around and run for the exit, and made her way down the long ramp to the door of the plane.

"It's my first time," she blurted to the flight attendant who greeted her. She'd said it too loud, and the woman's dark eyebrows jumped up like Rowan had startled her. Reading her nametag, she murmured. "Sorry, Nancy."

The woman smiled and pushed a fallen strand of hair out of her face. "Are you the dragon?" she whispered with a worried moue to her lips.

Rowan looked around at the passengers in first class. Two of them were staring intently at her.

Rowan nodded.

"No trouble on this flight, okay?" the attendant said in a barely audible murmur. "It's been a long week, and I just need this flight to go okay. Please?"

"Is there liquor on the flight?" Rowan winced at her own question. She wasn't the best at social situations.

"I'll bring you something to take the edge off. Is a mimosa okay?" the woman asked.

"Perfect. Can you make it strong?"

"Sit down so we can take off," a rude asscrack in seat 2A called out.

"Go on, and I'll bring your drink in a minute," the nice stewardess said.

"Great." Rowan had almost made her way out of first class before she remembered her manners and called, "Thank you, Nancy!" too damn loud again.

Asscrack shushed her.

Inner dragon growled.

Everyone was staring.

She tripped on a purse strap in the aisle and knocked a guy in 3C on the head with her carry-on bag.

He said the F-word and then called her the C-word.

She was *not* getting Damon a birthday present next month.

Why were planes so damn tiny? Everyone was mushed in here like a box of toothpicks, and the man in row five smelled like peanut butter.

Rowan checked the seat number on her ticket again. Every seat looked full from here.

"Hi," she said to a little girl who was flopped sideways out in the aisle as though she was already bored. But then Rowan felt bad giving special treatment to her, so she said, "Hi," to the next row, and the next, until someone sighed an annoyed sound from a window seat.

She missed Damon's Mountains already.

Behind her, Nancy was already doing the plane safety lesson, and Rowan really needed to pay attention to this in case of imminent death. She double-timed it to the back of the plane, which was apparently where her seat was. But when she made it to the single empty aisle seat, she lurched to a stop. Tall Dark and Mysterious was slouched down in the seat next to hers, looking out the window, the wires of earbuds snaking from his phone to inside his hoodie. *Oh my gosh, oh my gosh, oh my gosh, be cool!*

"Are you stalking me?" she joked.

He rolled his head on the seat and frowned up at her. Slowly, he plucked the earbuds away from his face. "What?"

"I said are you stalking me?" Rowan grinned, waiting, but he wasn't smiling. Another grumpy human then. "Never mind." She opened up an overhead bin and wrestled her small carry-on bag up there next to his black duffle bag. They looked cute together. Neon pink and black. She should take a picture for Willa.

Rowan pulled out her phone and snapped a quick one, then nonchalantly pointed it at Tall Dark and Mysterious, too, but before she could push the button, he shoved the flat of his palm in front of the lens and blocked her shot.

"What the hell," he gritted out. "No pictures."

"Oh, are you famous?" she asked, sitting beside him. "Are you a singer? You have lots of tattoos. I'm nervous." Rowan looked up front to see if Nancy had finished the safety lecture. Crap, now she was screwed if the plane went down. "Do you ride a motorcycle? You look like you would ride a motorcycle."

"Are you going to talk the entire time?" a man across the aisle asked. "I mean seriously. You're worse than a crying baby right now."

She narrowed her eyes at him. To Tall Dark and Mysterious, she lowered her voice slightly and said, "I forget how fucking grumpy humans are."

He had tucked his hands in his pockets and was currently staring at her. At least she thought he was. The damn sunglasses were hiding his reactions.

"Do you want to take a selfie with me?" she asked politely.

"No."

"I'm getting a mimosa." Rowan craned her neck,

but Nancy had disappeared.

"Probably not. Those are for first class."

"Nancy said she would bring me one, and I trust her. She has nice eyes." Rowan arched her eyebrows primly at his sunglasses.

Tall Dark and Mysterious scooted farther away from her and gave his attention to the runway again. Boring view, but okay.

Aunt Willa would freak out if Rowan sent her a picture of this guy. For years they'd played "I spy the hottest guy" but the pool was limited since neither one of them liked to leave Saratoga. Uncle Matt thought it was funny and even sent occasional pictures of guys for the contest. They were usually shaped like bath sponges and had armpit-stains, but probably Uncle Matt just didn't understand how the game was played.

The engines turned on, and the plane started moving. This was really happening. Panicking, she buckled her seatbelt and gripped the edges of the armrest as she panted loudly like an overheated German Shepherd.

Out of the corner of her eye, she could see the man toss her a look, but whatever helped her get through this, she was gonna do it.

"Miss, are you okay?" a kind lady across the aisle asked. "Do you need a barf bag?"

"This is my first time. This is my first time," she chanted as the plane made a wide turn. They weren't even going fast but inside, her dragon was writhing and uncoiling in anticipation. She apparently didn't like to give up control when they flew. *Don't Change!*

"Lady, settle the fuck down," he muttered beside her. "It's just flying."

"The second you fall asleep, I'm going to take a picture of you." Shit. *Stop panic-talking.*

"I'm not going to sleep then. Do you want to sit by the window?"

"Does it help?" Too loud!

"Shhhhh!" the angry human across the aisle said.

"I've literally had bigger shits than you," Rowan told him. In dragon form. The guy looked grossed out, but beside her, Tall Dark and Mysterious snorted.

The plane was going faster, and where the hell was Nancy with the mimosa? Rowan had trusted her. Trusted her with everything she had, and Nancy With The Kind Eyes And The Pretty Promises was failing her.

Rowan was breathing too loud now, and the rhythmic moaning sound that was filling the plane, she was mortified to realize, was coming from her.

"Jesus," he cursed, yanking her from the seat and into his. He stepped over her, lost his balance, and before she could stop herself, Rowan squeezed his tight little ass to try to help him stay upright. It was as firm as steel and round like a ripe apple, and she wished he wasn't swatting her hand away.

"Lady, stop it," he gritted out, clenching her wrists. He sat heavily in her old seat. Oh, he was a lot stronger than she'd imagined. That man could probably fondle the hell out of a dragon shifter boob. "Stop groaning. You sound insane, and you're scaring people."

The plane picked up speed, plastering her back against the seat, and outside the window, the runway was blurring past them.

"You said the window seat would be better!" she shrieked.

He hunched his shoulders as though the pitch of her voice had hurt his ears and clamped his hand over her mouth. In self-defense, she licked his hand and immediately regretted it. Squeezing his butt was one thing, but licking was taking it too far.

Especially since he gritted out in a terrifyingly deep voice, "That's enough, Bloodrunner."

Rowan froze, her tongue against his palm. Slowly, she retracted it and pursed her lips.

Finally, the plane leveled out, and the seatbelt sign overhead made a pretty *ding* sound.

"Mimosas," Nancy said from behind him.

Carefully, he removed his hand from Rowan's face and reached for the flutes of orange juice and champagne. Nancy gave him a wide-eyed smile that said, "good luck with this one," and made her way back to the front.

He handed her both drinks, but she shook her head and only took one. "That one is for you."

"I don't drink this shit," he murmured.

"We can pretend we are sitting in first class and take a selfie," she suggested.

He inhaled long and deep, then sighed it out like he was controlling his anger. "Fine."

Terror forgotten, Rowan grinned brightly and lifted her phone in front of them. With a pretty *tink* of their glasses, she snapped the picture. In it, she was resting her head on his shoulder with the happiest smile, but he was nestled deep in his hoodie and looked like he hated everything about his life. That just added to his sexiness. For reasons beyond her understanding, Rowan had a brand new thing for dark and broody, tatted up and moody.

She sipped her fancy drink with her pinky up. "I'm Rowan."

"I know," he muttered.

"How did you know I was a Bloodrunner Dragon?"

He took his mimosa like a shot. "Your eyes give you away, princess."

She grimaced at the nickname. "My friends call me Roe."

"We aren't friends. I'll stick with princess."

"Fine. What do people call you?"

He stared at the seat in front of him. He couldn't ignore her the entire plane ride, though, so she leaned her elbow on the seat, rested her chin in her palm, and waited. Tall Dark and Mysterious shook his head and gritted his jaw so hard a muscle twitched there.

"Kane." He cast her a quick glance, then lowered his voice. "People call me Dark Kane."

"Oooh, sexy."

"Not sexy. I hate it." He was untangling his headphones now, and she could see the shutdown coming from a mile away.

"What's your favorite thing about flying?"

Kane cast a long glance past her to the sky. "Sitting by the window."

Rowan frowned. And he'd given up his window seat for her? "Why?"

Kane made a *tick* behind his teeth and pushed the earbuds into his ears. And right before he turned up the volume and drowned her out completely, he said, "Because it makes me feel like I'm flying."

TWO

Kane hid his smile as Rowan Barnett told everyone around her goodbye—individually. She'd successfully driven everyone sitting around them on the second plane insane with her nervous ramblings.

Especially him.

Nah, that was a lie. Kane found her amusing as hell, and a great distraction from the long plane rides. Since he couldn't fall asleep at the risk of her taking more damned pictures, he had eventually turned down the volume on his music and listened to her unload a fireworks show of life stories.

She'd panicked again when they'd switched onto the small prop plane in Charlotte, North Carolina, and surprise surprise, they happened to be sitting right next to each other again. He smelled a rat, and that rat was a fire-breathing Bloodrunner Dragon named Damon Daye.

"I'm sorry I touched your ass and licked your hand on our first flight," Rowan said from behind him, way too damn close. Normally, he liked a lot of personal space, but his instinct wasn't even to run right now. He blamed that on the amount of time he'd spent beside her today. *Right* beside her since she'd fallen asleep on his shoulder for the last short flight. Didn't even try to use the window, just plopped her cheek onto him and announced, "I'm tired, night night."

Kane cleared his throat gruffly. "It's fine."

"So you forgive me for freaking out? Sorry ma'am. I didn't mean to get you. Oh! I'm making it worse. Sorry." Rowan was wrestling with her carry-on bag, which was eye-scorching pink like her ripped-up shirt. She'd turned the damn thing into a weapon and was pinball-whacking everyone around her.

To save her from yet another verbal lashing, and to save the other passengers from concussions, Kane turned and yanked the bag from her grip. "I've got it."

"Gentleman!" she exclaimed with a boner-inducing smile.

Kane snorted and looked straight ahead, shaking his head for the fiftieth time since he'd gotten on the plane. No one had ever accused him of being a gentleman. This lady was a trip.

Why was the line going so damn slow? These people needed to hurry up and get off the fuckin' plane already.

As much as she seemed harmless, Rowan housed one of the biggest dragons left on earth. It made his hair lift on the back of his neck to have her behind him. Even bubbly, she made the air like cement in his lungs. The humans probably didn't even know they were in the presence of a monster. That's what she was. He'd seen it in her eyes when she was having that panic attack. They'd turned the color of melted gold, and her pupils had elongated like a snake's. And she'd smelled of smoke and death.

Whatever she was doing in Asheville, he didn't like it. Rival dragons in his territory didn't bode well for him. Any blood relative of Damon Daye was a direct threat to Kane. Rowan could very well be the end of him.

He moved off the plane with the crowd and handed her bag back. God, what an awful color. He couldn't even look at it. Rowan walked beside him, practically bouncing with every step, which was really distracting because she was wearing a non-padded strappy sports bra under the ripped-up tank top, and her tits were bouncing. He could be fucking mesmerized by them if he didn't keep his head. His big one. His smaller head was apparently already devoted to her and getting harder by the minute. He needed to get away from her, and fast.

"Have a nice life, Bloodrunner," he muttered, ticking his lips up in a quick, empty smile for her.

Rowan shouldered her bag and kept in step with him. "So do you live in Asheville?"

Kane sighed and squeezed his eyes closed so he would stop staring at her tits. "What?"

"Asheville. Do you live here? It's a really small airport, way smaller than the other one. How do we get our bags? I have to get my suitcase as fast as possible. Guess why."

"I don't want to."

"Just guess! It'll be fun."

"Woman, I'm tired and ready to get on the road,

and I don't want to play whatever game you're running." Plus, his boner was getting worse, and people were going to be able to tell soon. He adjusted his hoodie over his dick and walked faster.

Rowan had the legs of a fuckin' gazelle, though, and sped up right along with him. He growled and rounded on her. "Are you here to kill me?"

Rowan ran into him. "Shit, Kane, you can't stop that fast in front of me. I'm clumsy as—wait, what? Why would I kill you?"

"Did Damon send you?"

Now she looked baffled. And beautiful. She was tall and blond, just his fucking type. Her hair was piled up on her head in a messy bun, and her cheeks were freckled. She wasn't a stick either. She had those fuck-me curves, soft tits, and an ass that would feel just right in his hands. Big blue eyes, pixie lips, and her lashes were dark. Hell, if she was some human tailing him, he'd have taken her in the bathroom and had her panting his name in no time. But she was Rowan Barnett. She was untouchable. She was a quick death by fire.

She was his assassin.

"Look, it's too big a coincidence that you sit in

the seats right next to me on both planes from Damon's territory to Asheville. Out of all the flights in the entire world, you land on mine? No. Why the fuck are you so intent on talking to me? On getting closer? On asking me questions and taking pictures?"

Her sandy blond brows had lowered the more he talked, as if his words were hurting her, but she was a dragon. She wasn't this ditzy, bubbly shell she pretended to be. It was cute as hell, but that was the lure, right?

"I don't understand. Do you know Damon?"

Kane huffed a humorless laugh and strode off. He wasn't going to listen to bullshit. Whatever she was getting at, he wasn't playing.

"You're being really mean." Rowan sounded confused, but at least she didn't sound right in his ear anymore. At least she was backing off.

He needed that because, right now, his chest and head were buzzing with some strange sensation that made everything blurry. It was like anger, distrust, want, hope, despair, and desperation all rolled into one, and for what? She would be out of his life in twenty minutes. All he had to do was grab his suitcase and leave her ass here to do whatever she was going to do in this territory.

His fucking leg hurt. It was that bone deep burn that wouldn't go away, but it was always worse after sitting down for a long time. Rowan was probably watching him, and he hated that. Hated that she was witnessing how weak he was, and he couldn't do a goddamned thing about it. Everybody stared. He wished he could stop limping, but it was impossible. He'd done the physical therapy.

This was as good as he got.

Kane pulled the hood of his sweatshirt farther over his head and ducked his chin to his chest so he could avoid the hell out of the stares as he made his way to baggage claim. When the chills lifted on the back of his neck again, Kane turned suspiciously. Rowan was following him at a distance, her chin tucked, her neck exposed. Those fucking gorgeous baby blues looked all sad and made him want to…want to…fix…something.

"I'm not trying to stalk you. I just don't know where to go," Rowan called, slowing even more.

Kane turned back around and did his best to ignore the instinct to duck out the side door and forget about his luggage.

He didn't understand her. He knew the facts—Rowan Barnett, age twenty-five, the only daughter of the Gray Back alpha, Creed, and his mate Gia. Beast Bloodrunner dragon, as big as Damon's monster, and a fire-breather and lava-spewer to boot. She was one of the last great beasts of the skies. Went to school in Damon's Mountains, didn't go to college, never moved away from her crew. That was all he'd been able to dig up when he was familiarizing himself with his enemies. She'd stayed at the heart of Damon's Mountains her entire life, and now she was here, in his territory, making no damned sense. The titan she hid shouldn't be caged by this bubbly, submissive personality. It had to be a lie. She was an actress and deserved a standing ovation.

There was a hundred percent chance she was sent by Damon to gather info on him, or outright kill him. Maybe it was because he was of breeding age now. He could spread Blackwing dragon genetics. Maybe. He didn't know. Damon didn't understand Kane wasn't a threat to him or anyone else. Not anymore.

He wouldn't risk putting The Darkness in a kid, and besides...he wasn't the kind to pair up. His life was a disaster, and he was an asshole, but he still had his head on straight enough. He wouldn't ever hurt a woman by tethering her to him. He was doing the world a favor by staying alone, so why was Damon threatened now?

And why the fuck had Damon Daye sent Rowan to hunt him?

He'd been sharing territory with Harper Keller for months and hadn't ever posed a threat, but then Rowan ends up in the seat next to him? No. This reeked of Damon intervention. Fate was a lie, and Rowan crashing into his life like a giant blinding meteor didn't happen without help.

Kane was being set up.

He waited for his suitcase on the opposite side of the baggage claim from Rowan. It took forever. Almost everyone had picked up their luggage and gone by the time his came out. God, he had to piss. He was so tempted to hold it, but it was a long-ass drive from Asheville to Bryson City.

Rowan was still waiting, the last one here, looking panicked. As Kane made his way to the restroom, he could hear her voice echoing after him as she asked someone if there were any more bags coming.

Not his problem, not his concern. The last damsel in distress he had tried to help, his entire life had been ruined.

But when he got out, Rowan was still at the baggage claim, and now she was crying. She lifted her eyes up to him hopefully, but he ripped his gaze away from her. He wasn't falling for this shit. He gave a two fingered wave and strode out the exit. But as he walked along the wall of windows toward the parking lot, Rowan didn't look like someone who was playing damsel. She broke down. Just...shoulders shaking, sobbing, looking around for help, but it was late, and that was the last flight, and no one was in this part of the airport.

She'd told him to guess what was in her suitcase, and now a sick feeling unfurled in his gut.

He stopped in front of the window and just watched her. Again and again, she checked the mouth of the baggage claim, but the lights flashed twice, and the track stopped turning.

Kane let off an explosive sigh and glared at the parking lot. He was so damn close to freedom. Shaking his head again, he limped back inside.

"What's in the case?" he asked her.

Rowan sniffed and spun around, and damn, the look on her face gutted him. He'd never seen someone look so scared. Not since Jeremy Jacob. Bile crept up the back of his throat just thinking about the kid.

Two more tears streamed down her cheeks as she stammered, "M-my treasure is in one of my suitcases."

"Shit."

"I have to have it. I'll get sick without it. The Sickening. I have to have it. I need it or I'll die." She sounded utterly panicked, and he got it. He'd seen Harper Keller when she was still undergoing The Sickening before she found her treasure. She'd smelled like blood and death. Just the thought of Rowan suffering the same slashed an unexpected pain through his chest.

"Come on. There will be someone working up front still. We'll see where it is. They'll be able to find it."

THREE

"But you don't understand. I need it," Rowan explained to the tired looking man behind the desk.

"Miss, I understand the bag is important to you, but it will take time to track it down. I simply don't have it here for you. I wish I had a different answer, but I've been searching our system for nearly two hours now. It's late, and my wife has dinner waiting at home for me. The airport is closed, and my resources are limited. I will get back on this first thing tomorrow, the second I come into work. I'll call you the moment I have any information for you." He shoved a card across the countertop.

Rowan plucked it from the shiny surface and read the name aloud. "Gary Folsome."

"You can call me tomorrow and see if I have any updates on your bag. With the layover you had, though, I have two airports to search. It's not here. I've gone through every leftover bag back there."

Rowan's face crumpled again, but Gary had been nice and had tried to help. It wasn't his fault the bag was lost. Rowan nodded jerkily. "Okay. Can you point me to the rental cars?"

"Oh honey, the rental car counters closed two hours ago. You won't get one of those tonight."

Rowan's shoulders sagged. "Are you serious?"

"I'm sorry. This isn't your night, is it? Look, I would offer you a ride, but it's against policy. Your man can probably track down a shuttle service for you, though."

"My man?"

Gary gestured to Kane who was sitting on a bench seat across the hall and rubbing his leg as though it was aching. "I'm not her man," Kane droned without even looking up.

Hmm. Good hearing on that one.

"Thanks, Mr. Gary." Rowan lifted his business card up and forced a polite smile. "I'll talk to you tomorrow."

Rowan wiped her eyes before she went back to Kane. He already thought her weak and pathetic, and right now she felt like it. Her dragon had curled up inside of her and was practically weeping for her lost treasure. She was exhausted, and her face felt swollen from crying. Her head hurt something fierce, and her night was just beginning. Now she had to figure out where to go until the morning.

"You ready?" Kane asked in a deep, gravelly voice. He sounded whooped, too.

"Ready for what?"

"Well, you can't sleep in the airport tonight. Come on," he said, easing to his feet. He shouldered his duffle bag and hers and rolled his suitcase behind him, leaving her to trail after him.

"Where are we going?"

"*We* aren't going anywhere. I'm going to drop you off at a motel and get the fuck out of Asheville. Still stinks of vampires around here, and I'm ready to get back to my place."

"Wait, there are vampires here?"

Her voice had jacked up an octave, and Kane gave her the strangest frown. "There used to be, and what the fuck are you scared of? That's like a dog being worried about fleas. You're a fucking dragon, princess. Act like it."

"Rude. You don't get to tell me how to act, Kane Dunderballs Franklin."

"Not my name," he said without turning around.

Rowan flipped him off behind his back, but Kane immediately said, "I saw that."

"You know, you shouldn't call me princess. I could set you on fire and devour your ashes." Just the thought of being a man-eater made her want to gag, though, and Kane didn't seem to take her seriously. He just shook his head like she was an idiot. He'd been doing that all day.

"I don't have money for a motel," she enlightened him. "I have enough for a rental car and food for three weeks until I can find a job here. I can just wait on one of the benches outside until morning."

Kane tossed her a look and slowed, waited for her to catch up. "You're a Bloodrunner Dragon."

"So? Why do you keep pointing that out?"

"You being a Bloodrunner means you are blood-related to Damon Daye, one of the richest men in the world. And you can't afford a motel?"

"Damon has money. Doesn't mean I siphon it

from him."

"Why not?" Kane asked as they walked through the sliding glass doors and out into the cool, dark night.

"Is that what you think of me? You did your little Internet search on the Bloodrunner Dragons or whatever, and then you met me, and that's where your first impression went to? I'm just some mooch off my family? You have a mighty low opinion of people, Kane."

"Not low, I'm just a realist. You have a need. Damon has the money."

Rowan sighed. "It's not like he hasn't offered to dig me out of tight spots, but…"

"But what?"

Kane was so ready to judge her, it was hard to explain it in a way where he would understand her and not think her stupid. Which she was. Brains weren't her gift. But deep inside, she really *really* wanted Kane to think better of her. "You wouldn't understand."

"Try me."

And she wanted to. She wanted to let him in a little bit. He borderline hated her, but he was the first helpful person she'd met outside of Damon's Mountains, and Dad had always said, "Look for the helpers. Look for the ones who immediately put themselves out to lift someone else up. They're the good ones."

Kane was a good one.

"I couldn't be completely independent."

"What do you mean?"

"I mean, I had to stay with the crew I grew up in, in the mountains I grew up in, with the people I grew up with. But when I made my own money, I could live with that. I bought my own trailer, my own home, paid for all my own stuff, even if money got tight. And I'm no brainy girl, Kane. I didn't do college. I barely passed high school. I got my own job, though, not from Damon, and paid my own way, and I'll never ask anyone for money. Not ever. I might not be smart, or brave, or good in crowds, but I can pay for my own stuff."

Kane had watched her as she'd spoken, but he still looked frowny, as though she confused him even more. Dismay filled her. She had that effect on people, but it sucked that Kane was like everyone else.

"Fair enough, but you can't stay out here all

night. Security is pretty strict about lurkers. I'm tired and hungry, and I don't have it in me to worry about you finding your damn treasure or sleeping outside, so I'll pay for a room."

"Oh, no, I couldn't ask you to do that."

"Princess, after that speech, I know you won't." He clenched his jaw and gave his attention to a wall of windows. The acrid scent of anger filled her sensitive nose. "Look, there's nothing I'd rather do than get out of here and go home. It's been a long fucking week for me. But you're playing a mighty good damsel in distress right now and I feel...I feel...." Kane made a soft sound deep in his throat and then muttered the F-word. It seemed to be his favorite of all the curses. "I'll get me a room, and you can crash on the floor. It's not charity, so stop looking at me like that."

"Hmmm," she hummed with a smile.

Kane's lips pursed into a thin line. "What?"

"I knew you were a gentleman."

"Woman, I just told you I'm going to make you sleep on the floor."

"But the floor is warm."

"While I sleep on the bed."

"And the floor won't have any bugs."

Kane ran his hand roughly down his dark facial scruff and growled—growled! It sounded scary for a human. "I'm no gentleman, princess. I really wish you would quit calling me things I'm not."

"Well I'm not calling you Dark Kane."

"Well, maybe you should!"

Rowan crossed her arms over her chest and grinned as he opened the passenger side door of an old Bronco. She pursed her lips against saying *gentleman* again.

"Shut up," he muttered.

"You liiiike me." Rowan scrambled in and sang louder, "You li-high-high-high-iiike meee!"

Kane slammed the door beside her and tossed their stuff into the back seat like it weighed less than a booger.

"You're strong for a human," she said as he climbed behind the wheel. When she squeezed his bicep, he flinched away from her. "Do you work out a lot?"

"Yes."

"Is it so you can grow muscles for ze ladies?"

"No."

"Is it so you can look at yourself in the mirror a lot?"

"No."

"Is it to make up for a tiny wiener?"

"No!"

"What are your tattoos?"

Kane turned on the car and jerked the radio dial to level-deafening.

"I'll guess then. You like the ocean, so you've covered your arm in mermaid tattoos."

"I don't like deep water."

"I'm scared," she blurted out.

Kane pulled out of the parking spot, but eased to a stop at the main road. With a long, irritated sigh, he turned down the radio and asked, "What are you scared of?"

Rowan swallowed hard. "The Sickening. Dragon's die slowly if they lose their treasures. It's an awful way to go."

She thought he would ignore her again, but as he hit the gas, he murmured, "You won't get sick."

A warm sensation drifted over her skin and landed in her chest. "Promise?"

"One of us in in trouble here, Rowan, and I have a

feeling you know it isn't you."

She frowned and buckled her seat belt. He said weird stuff that she didn't understand. But Kane was a smart man. She could tell by the way he talked, and she didn't want to ask dumb questions. But some of his words were like riddles. He was in trouble and she wasn't? That didn't make any sense. His voice had sounded truthful, as though he believed what he was saying, but she was the one with the lost treasure. And even if she did find her treasure, there was a mountain of stress—literally—waiting for her in Harper's territory. Rowan was supposed to be the protector of the Bloodrunner Crew, and she couldn't even keep up with her damned luggage.

No. If one of them was in trouble out of her and Kane, it was definitely her.

FOUR

Kane pulled into a motel parking lot and stopped in front of the office. He threw the Bronco in park and shoved the door open, got out without a word.

"Should I come too?" Rowan asked.

"Do what you want," he clipped out, limping to the glass door. He threw it open and started talking with a bored looking receptionist. She was young, probably a couple years younger than Rowan, with strawberry blond curls and blue eyes that had sparked with interest when she looked up from the book she was reading. Okay then. Rowan shoved open her door and made her way inside. She didn't miss the disappointment in—Rowan squinted at the woman's nametag—Rhonda's eyes when she saw

Rowan.

"Hey sexy-potomas," Rowan said, slipping her arms around Kane's waist.

Kane froze like one of those Grecian statues with the fig leaves over their peckers. She bet he would need a palm leaf to cover his.

"What are you doing?" he asked in that sexy, growly voice of his.

Damn, he smelled good, like cologne and something else. Something yummy and manly. Kane was dominant for a human. She sniffed his hoodie once more. "I'm flirting." She smiled at Rhonda. "Flirting with my love beaver."

"Oh, God," Kane muttered, but she was pretty sure she saw a smile on his lips. "I need a room. Do you have any left with two beds?"

Rowan explained, "We need a room with two beds, because double sex."

Kane snorted, and now he was angling his face away from hers, but she could still see his jaw all swollen up with his hidden smile. He cleared his throat loudly. "Do you take cash?"

"Uuuh," Rhonda said as she eyed her computer screen. "Yes, we take cash, and no we don't have two beds."

Rhonda smelled like horny pheromones as she lifted a flirty smile to Kane.

When Rowan shoved her hand in Kane's back pocket, he yelped and flexed his butt. Geez, he'd been doing his squats.

"Rowan," he muttered.

"Hmmm?"

"Why don't you go wait over there so I can get this done?"

"I like it here."

He sighed heavily. "Rowan, unhand my ass."

"Fine," she muttered, making her way toward a rack of tourist pamphlets. She picked up one on white water rafting, and then one on zip-lining. The third one made her gasp. She pulled out the pamphlet for Big Flight ATV Tours. "Kane!"

Kane ducked as if she'd thrown something at him. "God, woman, do you have to yell all the time?"

"I know them!" She pointed at the picture of Ryder Croy and Weston Novak riding ATVs on the front page of the brochure.

Kane glared at it. At least she thought he did because he still insisted on wearing his sunglasses, even in the dead of night, even inside. "Cool," he muttered, handing Rhonda a few twenties.

"No, I mean, I *know* them." She stared in shock down at the picture of her childhood friends. "They're famous."

"You're just now realizing this?" Kane asked. "Ryder has a massive following online."

"You know them, too? Kane, small world! We were meant to be friends."

"We aren't friends."

Unperturbed, Rowan beamed down at the pamphlet. "Oh, right." Rhonda was listening. "We're lovers."

Kane groaned, and Rhonda looked weirded out. Rowan held up the Big Flight advertisement. "I'm keeping this because they are my friends."

"Okay," Rhonda said, her blue eyes giant and her delicate eyebrows arched up like the McDonalds sign.

Kane shoved his wallet and the room cards into his back pocket. "Sorry for all this," he muttered to the receptionist.

"Bye, Rhonda," Rowan said with a wave of her pamphlet as she followed Kane out.

"Bye," the receptionist said as Rowan bounced

out the door.

Big Flight. Weston and Ryder on a real picture. "Are these things in lots of places?" she asked Kane.

"Probably."

"Wow," she said on a breath.

"I'm starving," Kane muttered as he pulled the Bronco toward room 10B.

"Me too. I could eat three hamburgers. There is that diner across the street. It says open all night. It says so, look. Open all night."

Kane didn't say anything, though. He just parked and unloaded their stuff into the single room with the small bed.

"This is fancy," Rowan said, hands on her hips as she scoured the room. Sure, one of the desk lights was out and it smelled like mildew, but it beat trying to sleep on a bench outside the airport.

"What you said back there," Kane said carefully as he washed his hands at the sink. "That isn't going to happen."

"The diner? It's happening for me. I'm hungry."

"Not the diner, princess. The sex. That's not what I'm about. That's not why I brought you here."

"Oh, I know."

"Do you?" He turned slowly and rested his hips against the sink. Crossing his arms, he asked, "Then why were you acting like that?"

"Because I didn't like the way Rhonda was looking at you. I don't want to talk about this anymore." She rifled through her purse for a tube of lip gloss. Mom had taught her to never leave the house without it. "Tonight you're my hero. Not hers."

Kane huffed a harsh breath. "I'm Dark Kane, Rowan. I'm nobody's hero."

She disagreed, but he would only argue, so she slathered her lips in pink and shouldered her purse. "I'll buy you dinner if you spend eight dollars or less."

He stared for a while, as if he was going to change his mind and stay in the room, but at long last, he nodded once and peeled off his hoodie. His black T-shirt underneath came up with it. Rowan got a peek at a gloriously defined six-pack and a sexy V of muscle at his hips. His jeans hung just right around his waist, nice and low, and when his hoodie came off his head, his sunglasses went with it. She'd imagined he was hiding scars, but his face was flawless. He was all sharp angles and the perfect amount of facial hair, and his eyes… He wouldn't meet her gaze, but from here they looked like a strange, bright color she'd never seen on a human before.

Then, in an instant, his sunglasses were back on and he was straightening his shirt over his smooth skin. His hair was a lot longer on top and shaved on the sides. Pitch black tresses flopped over into his face. His arms were visible now, biceps and shoulders pressing against the thin material. One arm was bare, smooth and tan, while the other was covered in tattoos. Roses and skulls. Sexy. The skin was uneven in some places, though, as though he'd been burned.

Kane looked like a badass.

"Whoa," she murmured, staring at his perfectly puckered nipples poking out from his perfectly defined pecs. One slow blink later, and she forced her gaze up to his sunglasses. "You're pretty."

Kane chuckled a deep, resonating sound, but cut himself off. His dark eyebrows lowered as if he'd surprised himself with that sound. He cleared his throat and ran his hand through his hair like a total sexpot. "Are we going or what?"

Why were her boobs tingling? She'd never had a type before, but right now, she was pretty fuckin' convinced her type was Dark and Delicious Kane. She wanted to have his babies. Well, not really his babies, since childbirth was dangerous for female dragons, but she definitely wanted to purchase a puppy with him, or at minimum a goldfish named Kane Jr.

But he's human.

Inside of her, Dragon became somber and sad. Kane couldn't be theirs. Not ever. Even if he didn't say riddles all the time, or dislike her, he was fragile. She'd tried that before, fallen head-over-heals for a man who didn't match her, and they both got hurt. She wouldn't hurt Kane. Not when he'd done so much to help her today.

Rowan smiled sadly and followed him out the door. As they walked across the parking lot, Kane looked back at her twice. Yeah, she was dragging her feet now. She'd never felt a connection like this—confusing and overwhelming all at once—and it would lead to nothing. Dammit, okay, she was pouting.

He slowed and waited for her to catch up before he spoke again. "I've come to the realization that you have two speeds." Kane shoved his hands in his pockets and his jeans slid down farther, exposing a strip of stomach muscle and making Rowan feel like the whole damn world was unfair.

"What speeds?"

"You are a blur in fast motion, talking ninety-to-nothing, asking so many damn questions a person can't keep up, or you hole up into yourself and go still. You are either spewing your thoughts or lost in your head, and there is no in-between."

Huh. Well, that drew her up. No one had ever put a finger on her manic personality quite so quickly. Even with sunglasses and in the dark of night, Kane was seeing her more than most people ever had.

Rowan lengthened her stride and slipped her hand in the curve of his inner elbow. His muscles were hard as boulders and his skin soft as silk.

Kane flinched and tensed, but allowed the touch. He cast a quick glance down at where they connected and let off a sharp breath. "Bloodrunner, I don't know your end-game, but after tonight, I'm gone, okay?"

Rowan leaned her head against the strong curve of his shoulder and sighed. "I know. It's fun to be friends tonight, though."

"We aren't—"

"For crap sake, Kane. Just let me have this. It's the only thing keeping my mind off my treasure. Just pretend with me, okay?"

His Adam's apple bobbed in his muscular neck, and then Kane nodded once. "Fine."

"Kane?"

"Hmm?"

"Are you afraid of me?" His response mattered more than she would ever admit out loud.

He didn't answer her, though. Instead, he suddenly became really busy opening the door for her and finding them seats in the bustling restaurant. Even thought it was two-thirty in the morning, the local bars must've just let out because the place was hopping.

Kane took her hand and led her to a booth in the corner by the window. The diner was all checkered tiles and black tables trimmed with chrome. There were a bunch of pictures of famous people on the wall with autographs. Kane's hand was so strong and firm around hers, she was having trouble removing her attention from the place their skin touched. He hadn't flinched away from her heat. She ran a lot hotter than humans, and usually they felt the burn immediately, but not Kane. In fact, he ran a little warm, too. Maybe his nerves were damaged. The more she studied his tattooed arm, the less his injuries looked like burns and more like shrapnel scars. Perhaps he'd tattooed the arm to cover them up.

For some reason, that made her really sad. Scars were badges of honor where she came from, but it wasn't the same for humans.

Kane grunted when he sat down too hard on his side of the table. He grimaced in pain before he carefully composed his face again.

"Did you fight in the war?" she asked nonchalantly, lifting her menu.

"Yep."

"Is that where you got hurt?"

Kane inhaled deeply and rested his elbows on the table, clenched his hands. "Do you ever have a little voice in your head that tells you asking certain questions might not be appropriate?"

"Like one of them angels on my shoulder?"

"Yeah."

"Nope."

He stared at her for a full three seconds before his lips curved up into a smile. He fingered the corner of the menu and said, "Yeah. That's one of the places I got hurt."

"There was more than one?" Shit, one was enough, especially if it was war. That was a big one. Some of the shifters in Damon's Mountains had fought, and they came back with scars on their insides and their outsides.

But Kane didn't answer her question and instead asked one of his own. "Why didn't you ever leave Damon's Mountains?"

"Because I don't feel safe anywhere else." Rowan pursed her lips and dipped her gaze to the appetizers. She hadn't meant to admit that. Not to Kane. He already thought she was weak. "Why do you wear the sunglasses?"

"Because I want to."

"But I saw your face. You don't have scars or anything. You look…" *Perfect.* "I like the way you look without them."

The waitress showed up, looking harried and tired. They ordered drinks and burger baskets. And when a pair of cherry cokes sat in front of them, Kane asked something she hadn't been prepared for.

"What are you doing here, Rowan?" His tone was so deadly serious she nearly choked on the bubbles in her drink.

She couldn't tell him she was here to protect the Bloodrunners because everyone knew about the shifter crews. Harper's crew had been in the news several times, and there was always a big buzz when a new crew began registering to the public. If Rowan admitted that Harper Keller, alpha of the Bloodrunners, was pregnant, all hell would break lose. She couldn't shift as long as she carried the child or the baby wouldn't make it. Harper was grounded, no flight, no fire, until her little baby boy sucked his first breath of air. The Bloodrunners were down a badass dragon, and they had enemies. Werewolves, vampires, ravens, and God knew who else would come out of the woodwork to try to snuff out the growing crew if they found out Harper couldn't defend them.

Kane was staring at her, waiting on her answer, and he didn't seem the type to let shit slide. She couldn't wiggle out of this one. He was human and wouldn't be able to hear a lie, but for some reason, the thought of lying to him made Rowan feel sick to her stomach and lose her appetite.

No, she couldn't tell him the whole truth, but she

could give him part of it.

"I'm headed to Nantahala to join the Bloodrunner Crew."

One dark eyebrow arched up slowly. "To register with them?"

"No. I'm a Gray Back, through and through." She hadn't even considered registering to another crew.

"But you're dominant."

Rowan snorted and sucked a long sip of her soda. "Have you met me? I had a panic attack on a plane. I'm not dominant."

Kane angled his head like a curious animal. God, she wished she could see his eyes right now. The sunglasses were really starting to bother her. It forced distance between them, and it also put her at a disadvantage. She couldn't get a read on his face, but he could see every emotion flitter across hers. She had a terrible poker face.

"Your human side isn't dominant, but I'd bet everything I own your dragon does just fine."

She inhaled deeply and stirred the ice around in a circle with her straw. "Yeah, well, lucky me. Submissive human, dominant dragon. Whatever power that decided to put two complete opposite personalities in one body is a douchebag."

"You don't like your dragon."

"No. I would be human if it was my choice." Then she could fall in love with a man like Kane, settle down, have babies, and not worry about them killing her. She could be normal. She could live un-hunted. She could be happy.

He huffed a disgusted sound and leaned back in the booth, crossed his arms over his chest. He smelled pissed, but for the life of her, she couldn't figure out why. She was allowed to feel how she wanted to feel about her dragon. Her animal, her body, her experiences, and screw his rude opinion. Kane the Riddler was human. He was the lucky one, and he didn't even know it.

"My turn," she gritted out, her cheeks heating with the anger that was flooding her veins. Time for him to get the uncomfortable questions. "Why did you join the war?"

"Money," he said immediately. His arms tightened over his chest, though, making his muscles bulge. "I had a mom and three brothers to take care of. I got recruited on my twentieth birthday, ten years ago on Friday."

"Did you believe in the war?"

"Do you believe in war?" he popped off.

"I'm scared of war. I don't like fighting."

Kane jerked his attention to a couple making out on stools at the counter. "I believed in money. I believed in the protection I was offered if I fought."

"Protection?"

"Look, my mom was overwhelmed, had no help financially, and I could take care of her and my brothers. End of story."

Or the beginning of a story she wanted to hear. "Where was your dad?"

Kane swallowed hard and leaned forward again, elbows on the table, shredding a napkin between his fingers as he stared at the confetti he was making. "Like you don't know. My dad's dead."

"Oh, no. I'm so sorry."

Kane jerked his attention to her, and those dark eyebrows of his were lowered again like he couldn't figure her out. "Don't be sorry, princess. He would've been the end of the world."

Rowan could see the shock in her own face in the reflection of his sunglasses. Those were big words, and more than that, Kane had infused each syllable with heavy hatred.

"My father was evil—"

"Kane—"

"Listen. You should hear this. You should really absorb it before you carry out whatever task you've been sent here to do." Great, more riddles. "My father was evil. He deserved what he got, and I'm not pissed at his end. I'm not like him, though. Not anymore. Now, I'm just trying to make it day to day."

"I don't like this."

"Here you two lovebirds go," the waitress said in a rush, shoving both their burger baskets in front of them. She pulled a bottle of ketchup from her apron pocket. "You need anything else right now?" she asked, her frown on the table of drunk twenty-somethings a couple booths down.

"Nah, we're good. This all looks delicious, Marny," Rowan said, reading her nametag. People usually smiled if she used their name, and Rowan liked making people smile.

And there it was. Marny looked surprised and grinned. "Okay, hon, flag me down if you need refills. This place is crazy tonight."

Kane took a massive bite out of his burger, but

Rowan wasn't done with their conversation. She lowered her voice and leaned forward. "I don't like the way you think I'm here to hurt you. I don't hurt humans. I don't hurt anyone. I don't have it in me. Besides, I like you. You're my friend—"

"We aren't friends."

"Stop saying that!" Pissed, she threw a french fry at his face that bounced off his forehead.

Kane froze, mid-bite. Maybe he would look terrifying if his glasses weren't in the way, but mostly he looked shocked and silly right now.

Rowan snorted and pursed her lips.

"Don't do that again," Kane ground out.

Rowan lifted another fry threateningly. "Or what?"

"Or maybe I'll burn you and devour your ashes."

The threats of a wimpy human. She threw the fry, but Kane caught it so fast, his hand blurred. Whoa. Maybe he got his strength and speed from his time in the military.

She frowned. "Are you still active duty?"

"No. I was discharged," he said around the french fry he'd just shoved into his mouth. "Honorably for injuries."

"Your leg?"

Kane ignored her. How was he already halfway done with his burger in two bites? Rowan bit into hers and—*oh, my God, that's how*. It was insanely delicious. Kane watched her snarf her dinner. She would've been self-conscious if his lips hadn't twisted up into a slight smile as she'd dug into her fries. They were the crinkle cut ones that tasted like happiness.

"How old are your brothers?" she asked, wiping her mouth with a napkin.

"Half brothers. Different dad, thank God. They're dad was a dirtbag, but they're normal."

Normal? Weird way to put it, but okay. "How old are your *half*-brothers?"

"Fifteen, seventeen, and Jackson is about to turn twenty."

"That's a big age difference from you."

"Yeah, my mom wanted the second family. The first round wasn't so easy on her."

"What do you mean?"

Kane cleared his throat and arched his eyebrows high. "I wasn't conceived willingly, if you catch my drift."

"Oh, my gosh," she whispered. "That's awful."

Kane gave her an empty smile and pulled a couple of leftover fries out of her basket. "Thanks."

"I don't mean that you were born, just awful on your mom."

"It was, and she wanted a redo when she recovered from what my dad did. She found Rick, and they were married, had three boys. Rick was an asshole, left my mom and all his kids, didn't even look back, didn't pay her child support. I remember I couldn't wait until the day I turned fifteen because then I could legally get a job and help my mom out. I worked at this pizza place on the night shift for a year before…"

"Before what?"

Kane cocked his head again, staring as if he didn't understand her. Carefully, Rowan leaned forward and reached for his sunglasses. Kane caught her wrist fast, and in a grip so hard it ground her bones. He shook his head in a slow warning.

"Why won't you let me see you?"

Kane's lips ticked up in a feral twist, and his voice came out too low, too rough. "Because I'm comfortable in the shadows."

Chills blasted up her forearms. Maybe it was the

story of his father that had her instincts blaring, or maybe it was all the riddles, or perhaps, it was the dead monotone he'd used when he'd admitted to liking the dark. Dark Kane. The nickname made a tiny bit more sense now.

"Psst," someone said behind her.

Rowan turned to find one of the slurring guys a couple tables away staring at her with a big dumb grin. His two friends were snickering from the other side of the booth. Rowan narrowed her eyes at him and then turned back around to Kane. Drunk idiots with nothing to say. Just wanted to interrupt her.

Kane's jaw clenched once, but he took a long, final draw of his drink and then asked Marny for the check when she bustled by.

"Sure thing," Marny said. "I'll go grab it."

"Thanks," Kane murmured low, but then his gaze seemed to train directly over her shoulder again.

"Pssst. Hot girl. Do you like it in the front hole or the back hole?"

Seriously? These guys were ridiculous. Rowan stared at a tomato slice on her plate and clenched her purse in her lap. The food in her stomach transformed to cement, and her mouth turned dry as cotton.

"You okay?" Kane asked.

"Yeah, I'm fine. I just don't like attention like that."

"Pssst!" Something hit her in the back of the head, and an immediate rumble vibrated through her chest.

Rowan closed her eyes. *Easy Dragon.* They're just some drunk pricks looking for attention.

"Hey," Kane called out blandly. "Don't do that again."

"Ooooooh," the guy said. "Angry boyfriend. She must only like it in the front hole." More snickering sounded.

Marny returned with the check, but Kane asked her to hold up while Rowan dug the total plus tip out of her wallet.

"Thanks, Marny, you were really good at your job tonight," Rowan said, trying and failing to meet her gaze. She could feel the guys behind her staring. Heat flashed up her neck. She was a freaking dragon shifter—one of the biggest monsters in the world. Those men were nothing, no threat to her, so why was a trill of terror zinging through her body right now?

Because attention gets us hunted.

The memory of fire flashed through her mind. Teeth and blue scales and a pitch black grizzly charging right toward her. Rowan winced and shook her head hard.

"Come on," Kane gritted out, standing easily, like his leg didn't hurt anymore. Maybe the dinner had done his body well.

He offered his hand, the first voluntary touch. Rowan looked up at his face to make sure he wouldn't yank his hand away and make fun of her, but his mouth was set in a grim line and his body was humming with tension. This wasn't a joke. Not to Kane, and not to her.

"Don't leave," the guy behind them whined. "We were just playing. Stay. We'll behave, I promise."

Rowan slid her fingertips up his offered palm until the insides of their thumbs touched. He gripped her hand gently. His skin felt like hers—hot as fire. An electric current sparked between their hands, but it didn't hurt. It settled her dragon. Kane didn't flinch away from her heat like she'd expected. Instead, pulled her up out of the booth like her weight was no bother at all. Gracefully, he brushed his hand against her hip and moved her to his other side, placing himself between her and the drunk assholes as they passed.

Rowan saw it coming. She saw the man's foot slide out into the aisle right as Kane stepped down on his bad leg.

"No!" she said, reaching for Kane as he lost his balance. But he didn't need her help. He caught himself on the back of the man's seat and immediately pulled himself toward the jerk. Kane wrapped one hand wrapped around the punk's neck, and he lifted the other in a closed fist into the air, ready to hit him.

When Kane bent his knee and rested his bad leg on the bench to pummel the guy, something metal and shiny gleamed from the hem of Kane's jeans where his ankle should've been.

Kane was an amputee.

He was also now beating the ever-lovin' shit out of the buttface who had tripped him. She was tempted to let him go, but she heard the distinct crack of a broken nose, and Kane wasn't slowing down, even with the guy's friends hitting and pulling at him. Shit.

"Kane!" She pulled his arm, but the damn thing was made of steel. He shrugged her off like her grip was made of paper. What the hell? She'd never had a problem overpowering anyone before. "Kane, stop!" She encircled his waist, ignoring the men glancing blows off her, trying to drag her off, yelling at the tops of their lungs. It was chaos, but she had to get Kane out of here. She had to save the drunken idiot from Kane's wrath. She had to save Kane from himself.

"Kane, you'll kill him!" Rowan gritted her teeth and jerked on his waist as hard as she could.

Kane stumbled backward, and Rowan shoved herself between him and the others. Kane's sunglasses lay shattered on the table, his face twisted into a snarl as though he was some wild animal. His hair hung in front of his face, and his lip was bleeding profusely, made worse by his grimace when he jerked his gaze away from the men at the table. Away from her.

He muttered, "I'm sorry."

For what? She wanted to pummel the shit out of them, too. Kane shook off her hold and strode from the diner with no limp at all.

"That guy is one of those shifters." Asshole then pointed at her. "So is she. Look at her eyes."

Crap. Rowan scanned the room quickly, panting under the stares of the others. Marny touched her shoulder, and Rowan jumped. "Best be on your way. The police will be here soon."

"They should be arrested!" the guy yelled. Both of his eyes were swelling shut.

"You started it, Brenton!" Marny yelled. "You've been starting shit in my diner for two straight months now. About damn time you got your ass beat." Marny gripped Rowan's elbow and led her to the door. "Go on now before you have a mob after you."

"Th-thanks, Marny."

"Sure thing, hon."

But when Rowan looked into her eyes, Marny wasn't smiling anymore. She looked scared. Rowan's dragon eyes did that to people. About now they would be glowing and churning gold like the sun, and her pupils would be elongated.

The walk back over to the motel parking lot seemed to take an hour. She could hear police sirens in the distance. They didn't make her hurry. She had time—time which she needed to think. Kane had an artificial leg, and it was something he was obviously really uncomfortable with. Why else had he evaded the hell out of her questions about it earlier? But that wasn't the only thing that had her concerned.

That man in there was right. Kane couldn't be human. She'd felt his strength with her own hands. His power had rivaled hers, but he didn't feel like a shifter. She had sensed nothing supernatural about him. He didn't have a smell or waves of dominance like a bear would have. And he had to be a grizzly shifter—nothing else made sense. He'd shaken her off like she was air. Her. One of the biggest and strongest dragon shifters left on earth.

Dark Kane was hiding dark secrets.

FIVE

The door creaked open under Rowan's urging. The room was dark except for the single light over the sink at the back that illuminated the bed in a soft glow.

The room looked empty.

"Kane?"

"Don't come in here," he said in a voice she didn't recognize. He sounded like a demon.

Rowan looked back out over the parking lot to the diner where the cops were pulling up, lights flashing. Going inside with Kane didn't feel terribly safe, but waiting out here was definitely a bad idea.

Rowan eased into the room and squinted her eyes, letting her night vision adjust. "Where are you?"

A growl sounded from the other side of the bed, the guttural noise much too realistic. A damn shifter! Didn't that beat all? She'd spent the entire day with him and not even guessed he was anything other than human.

Rowan padded carefully around the bed and hesitated. Kane sat there, sans shirt, knees drawn up, elbows resting on them, hands dangling in front of his legs, muscles flexed, and his eyes glowing a strange green color. Eyes that he wouldn't let her see directly. The second she sat down in front of him, he angled his face away from her. This sucked. He still wouldn't let her see him.

"What are you?"

Kane adjusted the leg of his jeans to cover the hint of metal, but she swatted his hand out of the way. "I already saw it, and I don't care."

Kane huffed a disgusted sound. "Bullshit." He flipped his hair over to his other cheek, hiding his eyes completely from her.

"I don't! You having a bum leg doesn't make any difference to me."

"Yeah?" he asked too loud. "You aren't secretly rejoicing? Your job just got ten times easier. And it's not a bum leg, Rowan! It's fucking *gone*. It hurts all the fucking time, and it's not even there. It's like I can still feel it…burning. My nerves are shot—fuck! Just kill me already so I don't have to pour my whole fucking life story out for you, Bloodrunner. This sucks enough without you knowing how weak I am."

"I'm not here to kill you, Kane, you bulbous dumbass."

"Then why are you here?" he yelled.

"Because Harper's pregnant!" Rowan clapped her hands over her mouth and wished she could swallow that secret back down. She'd just betrayed the Bloodrunners before she'd even joined them.

Kane slid her a quick, glowing glance. "She can't shift?"

Well, Rowan was already going to hell, so she may as well do it thoroughly. With a deeply irritated sigh, she removed her hands and scooted closer until she was sitting right in between his legs. He leaned as far back into the side of the mattress as he could manage, but at least he allowed her this close. "I'm here to protect Harper's crew until she can call on her dragon again. As soon as she has her baby, I'll be heading back to the Gray Backs where I belong. Now let me see."

"See what?"

"You know what."

He worked that jaw muscle good, stalling as he shook his head like she was pissing him off. Whatever. If she was sleeping in a room with a man, she at least wanted to know what kind of man he was.

Slowly, she reached forward and cupped his cheeks. His dark whiskers rasped against her palm, and gooseflesh surged up her arms. Gently, she pulled his face to hers, but he'd closed his eyes.

"You know," he murmured softly. "You know what I am, right? You know, and this has all been some fucked-up game you've been playing. Some mind grenade you are about to pull the pin on."

"Riddles, riddles, but I told you I'm not a brainy girl, Kane. Open your eyes."

Kane slid his palms up her arms and gripped her wrists as though he was about to pull them away. But he didn't. They stayed just like that, linked, touching, connected as quiet seconds dragged on. His heartbeat sounded so fast, like a hummingbird's wings.

"Please," she whispered, stroking her thumb under his eye.

Kane opened his eyes, and the green color glowed fiercely, too bright to pass as human. It wasn't the bright hue that terrified her, though. No, her terror was from the long, reptilian pupils that constricted as he focused on her.

"Oh, shit!" Rowan released him and crab crawled backward until her head hit the corner of the wall. She had to get out of here! Rowan scrambled up and bolted for the door, but Kane was there, his giant hand flat on the surface and pinning it closed.

A soft sob left Rowan's throat as she backed into a corner. "Wh-who…what…what…?"

Kane canted his head like an animal, his eyes glowing just as bright on the dark side of the room as they had on the light. "You really didn't know?" He took a deliberate step closer to her, and she cowered in the corner, ducked her face away, gave him her neck. Kane was a monster. A monster just like her but worse. Kane could hide and pretend to be human. *Run!*

Kane's limp was back as he squared up to her. He wrapped his hand around the back of her neck, and this was it. He was going to strangle her. He was going to kill her! *Dragon!*

But inside, her dragon was quiet and still. She was awed.

"Look at me, princess."

Breath shaking, Rowan obeyed him, lifted her chin, and forced her eyes open. He didn't look mad. He looked...sad. "I'm not going to hurt you, Bloodrunner."

"You keep calling me that like you aren't of my clan."

"I'm not."

"B-b-b—" Rowan squeezed her eyes closed and tried again. "Blackwing?"

"Blackwing Dragon," he confirmed. But right when she thought he would shift his hand around her throat and choke her, his grip went gentle, and he pulled her against his chest. His arms slid around her shoulders, and he just stood there, holding her.

Rowan's body went into shock. That's the only thing that could explain her traitor hands sliding up the strong curves of his back and hugging him.

Softly he said, "I thought Damon sent you to kill me."

"And you still helped me?"

Kane laughed a dark chuckle. "Well, I didn't claim

to be smart. And you lost your damn treasure. By the way, why the hell didn't you put your treasure in your carry-on?"

"They wouldn't let me. It was too big."

"So everything you have told me is real. None of this is some fucked-up game to lure me into a trap?"

"No! God, I had no idea what you were talking about half the day. Fucking Blackwing Dragon. Are you going to kill me?"

Kane snorted. "Princess, you are perfectly safe from me. Trust me on that one."

"Trust you? I just saw you play punchy-punchy murder on that guy's face in there. Wait." She eased back and moved his chin to the side, examining his split lip, which still looked like it needed stitches. "Why aren't you healing? Why isn't your dragon speeding this up?"

Kane made a *tick* sound behind his teeth and jerked his jaw out of her grip. "I'm not like you."

"Okaaay," she drawled, nodding like a bobble head. "I have about forty-five thousand questions."

"I bet you do." He slipped his hands from her shoulders, limped to the sink at the back of the room, and began filling the bowl of his hands with water. As he washed the blood off his face, his back muscles worked gracefully. His tattoos stretched from the knuckles of his left hand up his arm and over his shoulder, but his back was smooth and ink free. Delicious man.

Her sex pulsed once like it was a hungry little clam. Of course she would be sexually attracted to the one person on earth she couldn't ever have. A fucking Blackwing Dragon! Their people were enemies. Had been for millennia. The war between Bloodrunners and Blackwings had annihilated the damn species.

But his ass looked so fucking firm, she wanted to bite it. She suddenly wanted to bite his bicep, too, and his shoulder, and those little indentations above his hips and maybe his bottom lip. Basically she wanted to eat him up like the psycho she'd apparently turned into.

With a slow, dazed blink, she said, "Question number one, do you always remove your shirt when you are pissed off?" If so, she would make a mental note to anger him often.

"There was blood on my shirt."

"Oh." She scrunched up her nose and sat on the edge of the bed. "Gross. Question number two, can I see your peg leg now?"

"What?" He shot her the dirtiest look she'd ever caught. "Fuck no. And it's a prosthetic leg, not a peg leg. I'm not a damn pirate."

"Come oooon," she begged, laying on her side on the bed. "I'm going to be imagining it all night, probably dreaming about it, and it'll be way worse than it actually is. My imagination is ridiculous."

"Hell no. I haven't shown it to anyone. And I'd appreciate it if you didn't tell your crew about this either. Or Damon."

"Why not?"

"Because I already have to fight just to prove I'm strong. I'm challenged all the time. Telling the world I'm disabled isn't going to help me. It'll get every asshole who wanted to claim they bested a dragon picking fights with me." He ran a towel over his face to dry it and turned around. The one light above him cast all his pretty muscles into deep, shadowed indentations. Now she wanted to lick him *and* bite him. What was wrong with her? She should be fleeing the Blackwing in terror. She'd heard rumor one still existed, and here she was, in the same tiny room with him.

Her survival instincts were broken.

"For the record, you sure as shit didn't look disabled tonight. It took all of my strength to get you off that guy." She cleared her throat delicately and picked at a long, loose thread on the comforter. "By the way, thanks for that. For defending me."

"The guy tripped me," he muttered.

"You were pissed off on my behalf before that, though. You told them to stop throwing stuff at me."

"Yeah, why were you cowering to humans anyway? I don't get it." Kane crossed his arms over his chest and studied her. "I don't get you."

Those four words hurt like lashes. "Welcome to the club." And no, she wasn't going to get into why humans scared her more than shifters. She wasn't about to share her deepest, darkest secrets with a Blackwing Dragon. She wasn't a brainy girl, but she wasn't dumb enough to sign her own death warrant either. Oh, she understood why he didn't want others knowing he was down a leg. Any sign of weakness for a shifter could tip the balance of safety and death. She wasn't exposing her weakness to him. Not tonight. Not ever. "I'll show you my boobs."

Kane's face went slack. "What?"

"Show me your prosthetic leg, and I'll take my shirt off."

Kane's eyes narrowed and dipped to her chest. Rowan grinned because he was actually considering it.

"Bra, too," he negotiated.

"Naturally. Can't see my boobs with my bra on. Do we have a deal?"

Kane was frowning hard and looked super suspicious. "Is this one of those things where you back out after I take my pants off—"

Rowan pulled her ripped-up shirt off her head, then peeled off her bra. She squealed, closed her eyes, and covered her boobs with her cupped hands. God, she couldn't believe she was doing this.

When she opened her eyes again, Kane was smiling bigger than she'd ever seen. He was stunning. He strode forward a couple steps and unbuttoned the fly of his jeans, arched an eyebrow seductively, and jerked his chin at her hands.

"Maybe we should turn off that light."

"Nooo, that wasn't the deal, princess." He flicked his fingers. "Nipples."

She giggled and eased her hands away, then laid

on her side and rested her cheek on her hand. "Now drop your pants, Blackwing, and show me that sexy bionic leg."

Kane's smile faded away, and he was now staring at her chest with an entranced look. She'd hypnotized him. Rowan jiggled her boobies around and laughed. He cleared his throat hard and looked down at his crotch with a frown. "Sooo, the leg looks rough."

"Is it green?"

Kane snorted. "No, it's not moldy, Rowan."

"Does it have tentacles?"

"Okay, okay," he said, that sexy smile returning. Kane pushed his pants down and stepped out of them.

She wanted to take all of him in, so Rowan sat up in bed and worked her gaze from top to bottom. His dark hair was tossed to the side, covering his right cheek, and his glowing eyes watched her carefully. His muscular neck dipped down to defined pecks, and his perfect nipples were drawn up tight as if the cold air from the vent was getting to him. His arms were massive, like two sledge hammers ready to do some serious damage, and his abs flexed with every shallow breath he took. He wore briefs—black, sooo shocking—and one leg was powerful, big, and defined. But his other leg was thinner, tapered at the knee, and disappeared into the cradle of a metal prosthetic. On that leg, there were deep scars that stretched from his knee up his thigh, and they looked red, and painful.

"Does it hurt?"

Kane adjusted his massive erection and winked. "It doesn't right now."

Rowan giggled. Of course the man would find an innuendo at a time like this. "Is it from combat?"

Kane nodded once, slow. He made his way to the bed, and she was enamored with the way the leg moved with him. He had really good control of it, even though he limped. He sat down right beside her. "I haven't ever come right out and showed this to anyone."

Rowan brushed her finger up the metal. It was cold to the touch, the complete opposite of Kane's dragon-heated skin. He flinched, as though he would pull away, but he held his ground.

"How did you sleep with women?"

"God, Rowan. Filter."

"I'm serious. I've never met anyone who was

missing a limb. How did you hide it when you were…you know…banging shifter groupies?"

Kane leaned back on his locked arms and stared up at the ceiling. "I left my clothes on."

"Like you dry humped them?"

Kane let off a booming laugh, his abs flexing with it. "No, I didn't *dry hump* them. I can fuck a girl just fine without taking my jeans all the way off. I just need them low enough to pull my dick out."

"Sounds romantic."

"Well, when I got desperate, it didn't happen in the most romantic places."

"Like where?"

"Uuuh, in a bar bathroom or out in the back of my Bronco. Up against the wall behind this pizza place in Bryson city. And then—"

"Okay, that's good." Her blood was starting to boil at the stupid pictures he was painting.

"Are you getting jealous?"

"No. I just don't want to hear about the million women you fucked in every bathroom you encountered." Rowan plopped onto her stomach to hide her breasts from him and buried her face against the mattress to try and purge the dumb mental images from her head.

Kane's light touch brushed slowly down her spine, trailing fire where his fingertip met her skin. "It wasn't millions," he murmured. "It was six since I lost the leg. It was always after a fight, or when I was so fucking desperate to feel something…anything. And then afterward, I always had this awful, hollow feeling. It was like I was even emptier than before."

Rowan rested her cheek on her arm and traced the deep scars on his injured leg. "I hurt someone I loved."

"What do you mean?"

"I mean, I thought I found my mate. He was human, lived down in Saratoga, so not too far from Damon's Mountains. He worked at the newspaper. Brainy. Too smart for me, but he never made me feel dumb. He made me feel pretty, and I liked the person I was around him. But we got in a fight one day over something so stupid. I don't even remember what. And he said he wanted to take a break. That I was too much for him. He didn't like that I was a dragon and that I didn't know who I was. He didn't like that I couldn't leave Damon's Mountains. He said he didn't understand me, and it made me so mad.

Just…furious."

"You Changed?"

Rowan ducked her chin once as a tear slid out of the corner of her eye. "Too close to him, and he almost died. And the first thing he did when he woke up in the hospital was file a restraining order. And I was deemed a dangerous shifter. It's on my registration and everything. A permanent red mark that will follow me around for the rest of my life. I can't get a shifter grant for land of my own, and it's hard to find jobs. I barely finagled a plane ticket. So you see, I know what you mean by looking for something to fill you up, but being drained instead."

"Is that why you never left Damon's Mountains?"

"No. But I guess it's part of it."

Kane was still trailing his fingertip up and down her spine. God, it felt so good to be touched by someone who wouldn't break. Someone who understood her. Who wrestled with his own inner monster.

"Kane?"

"Mm," he grunted, pressing his palm against her back. His hand felt like fire there. Like he was burning his handprint into her skin, but she liked it.

"Who was your father?" She already knew, but she wanted Kane to tell her.

"Marcus."

The admission of his lineage broke her heart. Marcus, the alpha of the Blackwings. Marcus, one of the last immortal dragons. Marcus, the murderer of Damon's first mate, Feyadine. He'd ripped her eggs from her body and left her for Damon to find. And then he'd tried to burn the world. In an effort to save humanity from ashes, Damon had gone to war with Marcus hundreds of years ago. He'd thought him dead, but Marcus had only been badly hurt and gathering power, manipulating Feyadine's bloodlines to lure Damon into his final death.

Kane had been right. His father would've been the end of the world, but Damon had been the one to kill him. Rowan's great-grandfather had been the end of Kane's father, and a union between Bloodrunner and Blackwing would be her damnation. Falling for Kane would be betrayal to her family and her ancient clan. All of their deaths, all of their suffering at the hands of Kane's father, was too much for her to ignore.

But...

Even if Kane was a Blackwing, and there could be nothing between them tomorrow, it was nice to sit in this hotel room and pretend they were two normal people instead of two enemies on opposite sides of an eternal war.

It was nice to pretend Kane could be hers, if even for a little while.

Slowly, giving Kane plenty of time to retreat, she leaned her face toward his bad leg. His muscles didn't even flinch when her lips pressed against a deep scar there, but he relaxed instead and brushed his fingers through her hair.

He let off a soft sigh and murmured, "You're a strange one, Bloodrunner."

"My friends call me Roe, remember?"

Kane huffed a breath, but at least this time he didn't remind her they weren't friends, and that, to her, was progress.

Kane laid back on the bed and ran his hands though his hair, let the heels of his palms rest on his forehead as he closed his eyes. He drew his good leg up, the epitome of relaxed, but he wasn't fooling her. He was strung as tight as a bowstring again.

"Why are you stressed?" she asked, laying beside

him.

"Because you're going to be the death of me, and I like living."

"I am not. I already told you I won't hurt you."

"Yeah? But you're on a bed with me, tits out, and they're fucking perfect, and you just kissed my leg. You kissed my damn ruined *leg*, Bloodrunner. There are things in my life I couldn't believe happening to me, and that's one of them. And my dick is aching to just take you hard, but Damon will bring fire to me if I make bad decisions here."

"Gross. Let's not talk about Damon while I'm trying to seduce you."

Kane rolled his head against the mattress until he met her gaze. There, just slightly, was a smile in the curve of his lips. "You're trying to seduce me?"

Rowan waggled her eyebrows and beamed. "You won't even have to wear jeans."

That deep, sexy chuckle vibrated up his throat, and he shook his head again. Kane linked his hands behind his head and grinned up at the ceiling. "I bet you were a wild child growing up."

"You would bet wrong." She gave him a cheeky grin and repeated his words, "But you're on a bed with me, tits out—"

"Stop it," he said, but his smile was so fucking stunning. Straight white teeth and dimples she could see even under his dark scruff.

"Just so you know, I don't do this. I don't seduce boys wherever I go. I've been stuck in Damon's Mountains with the same silly guys I grew up with. And my ex and I broke up three years ago—"

"You mean you went dragon on his ass three years ago."

Rowan swatted his arm and rolled over on her stomach right beside him. "It's not funny to joke about that."

"It's kind of funny. So what you're saying is you are super deprived and sexually frustrated, and you'll take anything at this point."

"No! Kane, that's not what I'm saying at all." She made a frustrated noise. "I was saying I don't do this all the time. Ever really. I was trying to tell you that you feel…"

The smile disappeared from Kane's lips, and his eyes blazed brighter. "That I feel what?"

"Never mind. You'll just make fun of me."

Embarrassed, Rowan moved to log roll away

from him, but he caught her arm and held her in place, right beside him. "Say it, and I won't make fun of you."

His face was angled toward hers now, his lips only inches away, and her body was humming oddly from where his strong grip was wrapped around her upper arm. His blazing green eyes dipped to her lips. Kane was so big, so wide, taking up most of the bed already, and she'd never found a man more beautifully made than him. His pulse drummed against his muscular throat too fast, *bum-bum, bum-bum*, like hers.

"Tell me," he whispered, and she knew she was gone. She knew she couldn't deny him anything, but she couldn't understand why. Dragon wanted him. She wanted to sink her teeth into him and claim him so that he would never get away. She wanted him to choose them, because who else would make a match like this? Who else could hold their own against her? Who else could survive her if she lost control and Changed again? Who else had a monster that matched hers? Who else was this damn beautiful, this damn alluring, this damn everything?

Kane was big and important.

Kane was...

Closing her eyes like a coward, Rowan whispered, "I was trying to say that you feel special. I'm supposed to be afraid of you, but you don't feel scary. You're good."

"I'm not," Kane murmured, pulling her palm onto his chest, right over his racing heart. "I'm really not good, Rowan."

"I can tell you are—"

"You're wrong. I've killed people. I've hurt people, ruined people's lives. You shouldn't get attached to someone like me."

"But I've hurt people, too—"

"Not like me." Kane shook his head and leveled her with a look. "I'm not special, Rowan. I'm not important. Don't convince yourself otherwise, or I'll hurt you, too."

He was wrong. Kane didn't see himself the way she did. Okay, he'd killed people. War was ugly. War brought death, and he had been recruited to be part of that machine. But the Kane she saw—the one who helped her on the plane and at the airport, the one who picked up her plane ticket and who defended her at the restaurant—that Kane wasn't a pretender.

He'd given her real peeks into himself. She just knew it.

Before she could change her mind, Rowan dipped down and kissed him, her lips perfectly still on his. She hadn't done this in so long, and Kane lay like a fiery stone beneath her. They were both shaking like leaves, and she didn't know what to do now. Pull away? Maybe he didn't like this. Maybe this wasn't what he wanted.

Rowan softened her lips and eased back with a quiet smack. Kane's eyes were wide and so intense, as though she'd shocked him. Maybe he hadn't closed them during their kiss. His chest heaved with his breathing.

She'd just kissed the last Blackwing Dragon, and she should be terrified being this close to him. But instead, she felt safe. She felt happy, and deep inside, Dragon was practically purring.

Kane wasn't reacting, though. He wasn't blinking, and now a soft rumble was working its way through his body. With a baffled expression, he dipped his eyes to his chest. He drew a harsh breath, and the noise stopped. "What was that?" he asked in a ragged whisper.

His question hurt. "A kiss. I'm not very good at them. It's been a long time—"

"No, I mean...what was that noise?"

Rowan frowned. "That's your dragon, silly."

A loaded second passed, his eyes blazing and locked on hers, and then his lips crashed onto hers. He pushed and rolled her on her back, gripped her neck as his lips worked against hers. God, the man could kiss. He knocked the rust off her in three seconds flat, and then she was with him, kissing him back, making soft smacking sounds, making soft helpless sounds as her body lit on fire. And when he pushed his tongue past her lips, she was gone. Kane's body was graceful against hers, grinding once against her side before she turned toward him. Draping her leg over his hip, she gave him access, and he used it. He settled perfectly between her thighs and rocked his erection against her. Fucking shorts.

"I'm on birth control," she whispered, fumbling with her buttons.

Kane shoved her hand out of the way, slid his hand down the front of her pants, and *ooooh*. She rolled her hips to meet his touch. When Kane cupped her, slid his finger through her wetness, the feral sound was back in his throat. Sexy dragon. She'd never been with a man like this. One who she wasn't afraid of hurting. One who she could be herself with. He wasn't grossed out by her glowing eyes. Every time he pulled away far enough to meet her gaze, his expression became more determined, and it made her feel beautiful and sexy.

He'd found her clit, was working it gently while he swallowed her moans.

"Kane, please," she begged against his lips.

"Please what?" he growled.

"Inside."

Kane slid two fingers inside of her, stretching her with pleasure. God, this was too much. She was already close. So close, but she wanted more. Needed to touch him while she finished. Needed to bite him. *Stop it, Dragon.*

Rowan ran her fingertips down his chest, down his abs, down to the waist of his briefs and slid her hand into the band. His dick was thick and hard, swollen and ready for her. She eased out of the kiss just so she could watch his eyes roll back in his head when she gripped him. Kane didn't disappoint. How were his eyes so light? So bright? She drew a long stroke of him, and then another, and reveled in the fact that he was bucking against her now, their bodies crashing against each other like waves.

Rowan cried out as release exploded through her body, pulsing around his fingers. Kane was thrusting into her grip so hard now, so fast, like he was close, too. So damn sexy, but she wanted more. She wanted another orgasm, but better. She wanted him inside of her more than she'd wanted anything in her life. Rowan shoved her shorts down her hips in desperation, and Kane was there, on top of her, cradled between her legs, briefs shoved down his hips, his erection so long, poised at her entrance, and all he had to do was slide into her and end her agony.

But he stilled, arms locked on either side of her face, his triceps bulging, his eyes blazing like green fire, his black hair draped in front of his face, the swollen head of his cock resting against her entrance. Why was he stopping? No! Rowan wiggled lower, chasing him, but Kane flinched away, stumbled off the bed. "Fuck, what are we doing?" He was holding his chest as though he felt the same burning sensation that was filling her heart right now.

"W-what do you mean? I thought we were…"

Rowan sat up and covered her breasts with her arms. "I thought you wanted to be with me."

"I'm a fucking Blackwing, Rowan."

"So?"

"So you don't remember half an hour ago when you saw my eyes and got terrified? *Terrified*, Rowan. I could smell it on you. And now we're gonna do this?"

Anger blasted through her like a cannon ball. "You sleep with women in bathrooms but you don't want to be with me? I like you!"

Kane grabbed his jeans off the floor. "Don't, Rowan. Don't compare yourself to a quickie bathroom-fuck. You don't want to be one of those women."

"I do, too! I want you."

Too loud, he asked, "You want to be someone who adds to the emptiness?"

Rowan gasped at the pain those words slashed at her heart. In a rush, she pulled the comforter over her because, right now, she'd never felt so exposed, so vulnerable.

Kane only bothered with jeans before he strode for the door. He threw it open, but stopped before he disappeared. "Rowan, you and I can't be. We can't.

And I can't push us that far and expect us to be friends after. I made a mistake. I'm sorry."

In the instant before he let the door swing closed behind him, he lifted his gaze to Rowan's, and his eyes were so sad she had to look away. She didn't want to see that kind of pain in anyone, and especially not the man who already felt like so much more than a friend.

Something small and warm splatted against her wrist, but she knew what it was before she even looked down. A small drop of damning crimson sat on her pale skin. It had begun.

The Sickening was here, and it had reared its ugly head in the moment her heart had been damaged by Dark Kane. Warmth trickled down her lip from her nose, and a sob wrenched up Rowan's throat.

Her treasure was lost, The Sickening had begun, and she was alone, far away from the safety of Damon's Mountains. All she wanted was for Kane to hug her and tell her everything would be okay, but one broken dragon couldn't fix another broken dragon.

And Kane had made it perfectly clear.

They weren't friends.

SIX

Shit, what was he doing? Kane gripped his T-shirt harder and paced in front of room 10B. Everything in him, every instinct, every desire, wanted to go back in there and fuck Rowan. No, not just fuck her. She wasn't one of the other women she was comparing herself to. She was more. So much more.

He couldn't breathe. His chest was so damn tight he couldn't draw a full breath, and now he was panting in desperation. When a soft, heartbroken sound drifted from the room, Kane hated himself. Hated everything. Hated his past, hated his future, hated the man he'd become. Hated the man he was born to be.

Rowan was crying because of him. Crying over a man who didn't deserve her tears.

What was it about her? He'd planned on going to the pool and sitting in a plastic lounge chair until morning so he could give them both space, but here he was, staring at the window of their shitty hotel room, completely helpless to leave.

She'd done something to him. Bewitched him maybe. He'd never believed in that stuff, but Kane had known Rowan less than twenty-four hours, and she felt like the damn moon, and he was the tide, affected by her whims, her moods. If she'd told him to stay…if she'd demanded it, he would've. He wouldn't have been able to say no.

What the fuck was wrong with him? And why did his chest hurt so goddamn bad? He pressed his palm over his heart to see if his skin there was as hot as it felt. Another sob, and he couldn't fucking breathe! This wasn't how he'd seen the day going. It wasn't how he saw his life going. He was supposed to be alone for always, but Rowan came in, busting up his walls like a bull in a china shop. She'd shattered him in a day.

And the noise in his chest? The one she'd drawn

from him? That wasn't supposed to exist. He didn't control the dragon, didn't have access to The Darkness anymore. But there had been the rumble there, so familiar. It had felt like home, and something deep inside of him had told him Rowan was to blame, or perhaps thank, for a glimpse of himself again. He'd lost his mind in desperation to hear that sound again. To make that sound. He'd kissed her in a silent plea for her to fix what was broken inside of him, but Rowan didn't have that power. No one did. It wasn't fair of him to attach to her. It wasn't fair on her, and it wasn't fair on him, because the second she figured out what was wrong with him, and how weak he really was, how useless, she would leave, and he would be full of nothing but infinite hollowness.

Hope was a slow and painful death to a man like him.

He was a shadow, at home with loneliness. At home in the dark, but Rowan was light. She was happy and loved people. She was social and mirrored strangers' smiles without effort. She was jokes and laughter and constant happy chatter, and he was a stone gargoyle that would shroud her life in darkness.

He'd known her for less than a day, but already he wanted better for her. Tomorrow, he would take her to the airport, make sure she got her rental car, and let her go. And when she was safe, far away from him, he would go to work finding her treasure. He would make sure she was okay. And maybe when she was in Nantahala and he lived near, he would do little things for her to make life easier. Little things she would never notice. Pay for her drinks at the bar, or cover her coffee if she was in the drive-through behind him one day. Maybe he could put in a good word and help her get a job in Bryson City, so long as she didn't know it was his kindness helping her out. Rowan didn't need to attach, but he could tell here and now, as her soft sobbing shredded his insides, that she was his. Not his to keep, but his in the only way he could have a woman—from afar.

Determined not to listen to whatever instinct was screaming to go in there and fix her, Kane squatted down and narrowed his eyes at the door to 10B. He could still smell her on him. Rowan's pheromones had been off the charts calling to him, filling his head, filling his damn jeans. Here she was breaking down, and he was outside her room thinking about the way she'd felt when he slid his fingers inside of her. Of how she'd writhed against him and begged for more. Of how her mouth tasted and her hair smelled like roses. Of how gold her eyes had turned when her inner dragon was riled up. Of the easy way his fingers had slipped through her blond waves, the way her lips parted right before he kissed her.

She was inside, crying, and he was thinking about how fucking sexy she was. *Monster.*

Kane wanted to spit, but stood and linked his hands behind his head instead. His leg hurt again. Rowan had made it better for a while, or maybe it was the adrenaline from the fight, he didn't know. He wanted more relief, though.

She was inside crying, and he was wishing she could make *him* feel better. *Monster.*

Was it wrong that he already wanted her forgiveness? Was it wrong that he wished he could just walk in there and she would open her arms and pull him in close and tell him he wasn't an asshole? He was shit at apologies.

She was inside crying, but he wanted her to

siphon the bone-deep regret from him so he could breathe again. *Monster.*

Debating on going for a drive to clear his head, Kane grimaced at his Bronco, but when he did, his lip didn't hurt like it should have. Kane ran his finger over the split that asshole had punched into his bottom lip. He couldn't find it. Frowning, he strode to his truck and leaned down, searched for the cut in the driver's side mirror. Where the fuck was it? Rowan had been kissing him just as hard as he'd done to her, so it should be looking like crap about now, torn to hell and maybe still bleeding, but nope. The bruising around his mouth was already gone, and there was no split. Kane searched his face desperately, looking for any sign of the fight, but there was none.

Stunned, he stood up and stared at the door to the hotel again. His healing was shit, but Rowan had done something to him. Maybe kissing her had healed his face faster, or being around her, or…something.

She was a witch. That was the only logical thing that could explain the way he felt about her, and now this? Witchcraft. Some Supes had extra powers. Vamps did for sure. Super healing, speed, strength, agility…why would it be out of the realm of possibilities that Rowan was a dragon and a witch? There was heavy magic in the Bloodrunner line, and clearly some of that had passed down to Rowan.

Maybe that's why Damon had tucked her away in his mountains like a princess in a tower for all those years.

Kane should be wary as hell right now, but instead, Rowan had somehow demanded even more curiosity from him. That saying "curiosity killed the cat"? Well, curiosity was going to get his ass burned alive by Damon and eternity in the belly of the blue dragon himself.

Kane needed to get away from Rowan. He needed to separate them, put distance between them, and get ahold of his damn mind before he lost it completely. All he had to do was get in the Bronco and drive away. His keys were in his pocket.

But he couldn't. He tried, but he couldn't force his hand to open the door. Rowan was still crying, he couldn't move, and he was going to be pinned here all night, waiting for her to release the hold she had on him. And he still couldn't breathe.

He hadn't felt this powerless since that night at Jeremy's house when The Darkness had taken over.

But this was different. It wasn't The Darkness controlling him now. He was alone in this body. No, there was another dragon to blame for this paralysis.

Anger flooded him, black and roiling. He wasn't just some plaything.

Kane took a step toward the hotel room and then another. It was easy moving this way, he just couldn't move to escape her. Fucking traitor body was fine walking back into danger, but not to flee to survive.

Kane threw open the door, ready to strip her down for controlling him like this, but the second he did, the weight lifted as though it had never existed. His lungs filled with oxygen and he felt…relief.

Rowan had her back to him at the sink, her shoulders shaking with her crying. When she looked up at him in the mirror, his stomach dropped to the floor. The tissues she was holding up to her face were soaked with blood. Shit.

"You left, and then I felt something warm, and I already know what this is," she cried, her face crumpled and desolate. "It's The Sickening. I have to find my treasure, and no one can help me."

"Shhhh," he said, taking the tissues from her. "Let me see."

Her face was covered in smears of red, but her nose didn't look to be bleeding anymore. "Look, it's done."

"It is?" she asked in a pitiful voice.

"Yeah, princess. It's over. Tomorrow we'll track down your suitcase, and this will all just be a bad memory. You have time."

"How much?"

Kane shook his head helplessly. "It took months for Harper."

"Did she bleed this bad in the beginning? Did she get headaches?"

"I don't know," he whispered, wiping her face with a wet washcloth. "I'm not a Bloodrunner, and she wouldn't ever share that information with me."

"What about you?"

"What about me?"

"What is your treasure?"

That question gutted him. He would've given his other leg for the instinct to find a treasure, but he wasn't okay. "Princess, I'll never need a treasure, and I'll never undergo The Sickening."

Rowan's pretty blue eyes got so round. "Why not?"

And this was the moment when he admitted something awful. When he admitted his greatest shame. When he told Rowan just how beyond help he was.

"Because," he murmured, "my dragon was taken from me."

SEVEN

Kane's dragon was taken? Rowan didn't understand, but he'd cut off her questions as they'd readied for bed. His eyes had dimmed, and he had shut down. Now he was lost in his head, oblivious to everything around him.

Kane had taken one of the pillows off the bed and spread a thin blanket on the floor for himself, but while he was taking off his shirt, Rowan had pulled the pallet back up onto the bed.

"What are you doing?" he asked in a tired voice.

"Making history."

Kane sat on the edge of the mattress and unhooked his prosthetic leg. "What do you mean by that?"

"Think about it. Blackwings and Bloodrunners have been enemies for centuries, but here we are, best friends—"

"Acquaintances," Kane corrected her.

"And diddle buddies—"

"I finger-banged you once."

"And now we have two sides of an ancient war sleeping in the same room. Fate led us here, Kane. Let's snuggle."

Kane didn't even fight her, just set his prosthetic leg on the chair by the bed and climbed under the covers with her. "You're relentless," he muttered.

"Thank you."

"That wasn't a compliment."

"Would you like to be the big spoon or the little spoon?"

Kane's teeth flashed in a white smile in the dark. "Big."

"Fantastic choice. That way your wiener can touch my butt cheek." She rolled over and waited, not missing the soft chuckle behind her.

Slowly and carefully, Kane rolled toward her and hugged her back tightly against his chest. Indeed, his stony erection pressed against her butt. "This still doesn't change anything tomorrow."

Rowan yawned. "Technically, it is tomorrow."

"Hm," Kane grunted noncommittally.

Her eyelids grew heavy with the air vent blasting cold air onto her and Kane's warm, strong body pressed against her back. Even his knees were drawn up, touching the backs of hers. "Kane?"

"What?"

"I don't mind that part of your leg is missing." She bent her knee up higher, drawing her calf to where his shin would've been. "I mean, I wish you still had it so you wouldn't hurt, but it makes you unique. I've never met a man like you."

"You've never met a shifter without his animal, and a man without all his body parts? That's not shocking, princess. We're a rare breed."

Rowan rolled over in his arms and snuggled against his chest until he relaxed again. "You feel whole to me," she said sleepily.

Kane went quiet. She would've thought him asleep if he wasn't rubbing her back gently. He smelled so good, like lingering cologne and some masculine deodorant probably called Grizzly Motorcycle Pine Tree or something. His heart beat strong and steady against her cheek, and despite him being a Blackwing, she'd never felt so safe in the arms of a man.

He let out a long, steady breath, as if he'd been holding it for a while. "Rowan?"

"Mmm?"

"Are you magic?"

She smiled sleepily and kissed his chest right along the edge of his tattoo. Silly dragon. He was the one who had made her feel better after the terror of The Sickening. "No. There is no magic in me."

"Swear?"

Rowan bit him gently, then released his pec. She ignored her inner dragon's urging to bite him again harder. "I swear."

Kane swallowed audibly in the dark and whispered, "Night, Roe."

Rowan's lips stretched with a smile that felt so good. Roe. Not princess or Bloodrunner, but by the name her friends called her.

He'd just given her a gift. He'd just called her a friend and settled her sickly dragon even more.

Kane didn't realize it, but he was the magic one.

****

Three days. Rowan gripped the steering wheel harder and heaved a stressed-out sigh. Three days, and she would have her treasure back. The airline guaranteed it. Meanwhile, she didn't have time or money to hang out in Asheville while they looked for the lost luggage, so here she was, following Kane's Bronco in her rental convertible.

Kane turned off at an exit that read Bryson City. The GPS was telling her to follow the highway, but she hadn't said a proper goodbye to him, so like the stalker she was, she followed him off the exit ramp, down a few back roads, and into a gravel parking lot near an old-fashioned tourist train station. Two hours in the car, and she needed to stretch her back and legs. At least she hadn't had a bloody nose yet today. She didn't even have a headache, so maybe Kane was right. Maybe she had lots of time.

"Fancy meeting you here," she called as Kane got out of his Bronco.

"I'm hungry as fuck," he said. "Come on. I know a place with fried mushrooms that look like little dicks."

Rowan snorted. "You know the direct way to my heart. I was following you to say goodbye, though."

"They have homemade ranch. You can make it look like jizz on the mushrooms."

Well in that case… Rowan marched herself right on over to Kane and linked her arm in his. "Lead on, sexy dragon."

Kane tensed. "I don't like you calling me that."

"Well, you are sexy, so…"

"No, I mean the dragon part. I'm not a dragon."

"Your glowing dragon eyes say differently. Look at this sparkly rock." She stooped and picked it up, then showed him because Kane was being sweet and pretending to be interested. It glittered gold like fish scales in the sunlight when she turned it in her palm. "This is for you."

Kane's eyebrows lowered, and he took it slowly. "What is it for?" he asked suspiciously.

"To keep in your pocket so you can always think of me."

"Jesus, woman." Kane turned to the side and chucked the rock as hard as he could into a small grove of trees.

"Kane!" she yelled, instantly furious.

But when she looked back at him, he was grinning. He held out the rock, still sitting on his palm. The turd. She shoved him hard in the shoulder and didn't even feel bad when he went off balance and had to right himself on his bad leg. Rowan crossed her arms and marched toward the main drag. "I'm never letting you see my boobs again."

Kane was laughing now, and it made her even angrier. "Roe, wait." He caught up in front of an old-fashioned ice cream parlor and pulled her to a stop. Even if he was going to apologize, he was still smiling so it wouldn't count.

"I gave you a treasure, and you were going to throw it away."

Kane angled his head, dipped down lower so he could catch her averted gaze. "Stop pouting and look." He held up the pebble between his thumb and forefinger, then shoved it deep into his pocket. Right next to his obvious boner.

"Why are you turned on right now? I'm angry."

"Yeah, well…" Kane glanced around and adjusted his dick. "You're really cute when you're mad."

Rowan made an offended huff of breath. "Kane, I'm a *fucking dragon*, as you keep reminding me. I'm not cute when I'm angry. I blow fire, stomp on trees, and destroy stuff."

"I'll buy you lunch if you spend eight dollars or less."

She wanted to stay mad, but his stupid smile was so freaking handsome, and he didn't have smile lines either. His face was smooth as though he never grinned, yet here he was teasing her. "I'm gonna spend nine of your dollars," she sassed, turning on her heel and striding toward the stairs to the restaurant he was pointing to.

It was lunch rush, and the hostess told them they had to wait while their table was cleaned. It was too crowded inside, so Kane led her outside. Rowan rested her elbows on the railing that skirted the outside eating area. This was her first real look at the town. A train was blowing a whistle behind them, and a pair of jacked-up trucks were racing down the main street. Tourists were everywhere. She could tell they were tourists because they hauled souvenir bags and wore Bryson City T-shirts with little printed bear logos all over them. Restaurants and souvenir shops lined both sides of the street, and beyond the sleepy town, green mountains jutted up to meet the vibrant blue sky. It would be fall soon, and likely cold, but not today. Today the weather was perfect.

Kane leaned against the railing, mirroring her stance. "Is it a lot different than Saratoga to you?"

"Yes and no. They're both small towns and have the same sleepy feel. It's the mountains that are different," she murmured, staring at the towering hills outside of town. "Damon's Mountains are covered in evergreens."

"These will stun you in the fall."

"You like it here?"

Kane nodded. "I do. I've been trying really hard not to get chased out of Bryson City."

"Who chases you?" She would kill them. Kill them? Clearly she was losing her mind around this man.

"Kane, your table is up," the hostess called. She was setting a pair of menus on a table outside in the shade. "I think this is the first time I've seen you eat anywhere but at the bar inside," she said lightly.

"Yeah." Kane shot Rowan a frown across the table. "It's a nice day out here."

The waitress, Sandy, her nametag said, placed her hands on her hips and beamed at Rowan. "Two years eating in here, and he's never let me sit him anywhere but the bar. Same seat every time, too.

Right at the end, away from everyone."

That drew Rowan up short. How sad to want to be alone for all his meals like that. The server got their drink orders and scurried off. Rowan leaned forward. "Don't you have friends?"

"No," Kane said, void of hesitation. Then he lifted his menu in front of his face to show her the conversation was done.

Rowan snatched it out of his hands. "And who chases you?"

Kane growled and leaned forward. "Everyone, Rowan. The wolves, the vampires, the bears, panthers, lions, boars. Whoever settles a territory doesn't want a dominant shifter living there without fealty to them."

"But you don't have the animal."

"They don't know that, and it needs to stay that way."

"So many secrets."

"And I've trusted you with them."

"Not all of them. What happened to your dragon?"

"Nope." Kane sat back and lifted his menu in front of his face again, this time too far away from the table for her to yank away.

"I'm spending ten of your dollars now. Do you want to play footsies?"

Kane chuckled from behind the menu. "Play with my good leg so I can feel it."

And she did. Rowan rested her foot right inside of his and rubbed the toe of her sneaker against his heel. When Kane gave in and dropped the menu, the corners of his lips were still in a smile. "You don't care about personal space at all, do you?"

"No."

"Are you one of those girls? You know...the ones who need constant affection in a relationship?"

"Yes."

"Needy," he accused.

"Not needy. It's natural for shifters to crave affection. Even with my friends, I like to hug them or bump their shoulders or sit really close. I grew up in the Gray Back Crew, and we're an affectionate lot by nature. I'm not weird Kane. Maybe *you* are."

"The Bloodrunners are like that," he said so softly she almost missed it.

She wished he wasn't wearing the extra pair of sunglasses he apparently kept in his Bronco for when he got his smashed in fights. She wanted to see his eyes when he'd said that. The tenderness in his voice caught her off guard. "How do you know?"

"Because I watch them. I work with Wyatt, and I saw him before Harper came. I saw him before the Bloodrunners formed a crew. He was empty, angry, wanted to fight all the damn time. Now he's like one of those goats at the petting zoo. You know which ones I'm talking about? They just sit there, getting petted, looking all drunk and happy."

"I'll be sure to let Wyatt know you compared him to a drunken billy goat."

"You know what I mean. And when I see the crew at the bar, they are always touching. Even the ones who aren't paired up. Hugging and linking arms, like you do to me. It's…"

"It's what?"

"Unsettling. Confusing."

Rowan sighed and rubbed her foot against his ankle. "Does it feel good when I touch you?"

Kane shrugged one shoulder up and muttered, "Sometimes."

But sometimes not. That's what he was saying. Rowan frowned down at her menu so he wouldn't see the hurt on her face. It wasn't fair for her to get frustrated if he didn't like touch. It was his body.

"Kane, why aren't you in a crew?" she asked before she could change her mind.

He took a long drag of his water before he answered in a careful voice, "You know why."

"You're a shifter."

Kane's gaze tracked a woman walking close by their table. He clenched his jaw and leaned forward, then whispered, "I'm not. I'm just a man now. And I don't want to have this conversation again."

"My mom is human."

Kane leaned back in his chair and crossed his arms, angled his face like he was studying her. "So?"

"So she's a Gray Back just as much as me or my dad, or Beaston, Jason, Aviana, Georgia, Matt, Willa, any of them. She's crew. Doesn't matter that she doesn't have an animal in her. If you found a crew, no one would chase you anymore. You could be safe. You wouldn't be alone."

"Rowan—"

"You wouldn't be sitting at the end of a bar eating by yourself anymore, Kane. You would have people."

"Yeah, and when they need protection? When they need me to have their back? When they need my fucking dragon? I know how it is, princess. Crews bring battles. Territory disputes alone put the Smoky Mountains into chaos for months when Harper started setting up the Bloodrunners. When I let myself care for these people, let them in, and pledge my life to keep theirs safe, what do I do when it comes to war? I'll sit on the sidelines, helpless, crippled, watching my friends bleed, and I can't do a fucking thing about it. And even if I could, even if I still had my dragon—he. Was. A. Monster. You have it in your head I'm some worthy hero, Rowan. I'm not. I'm where I'm supposed to be."

"Alone?"

"Hell yes, alone. I'm happy like this."

"Are you?"

"Yes, woman. I'm not your project to fix. I have a good job, I have a routine, I have a house, I have my own life, and it's a good one. It's one I've carved with my own blood, sweat, and tears. It's one I've built from nothing, Rowan, *nothing*. I don't need you to swoop in here and fix me. I'm good. I don't want friends. I don't want a crew. Just"—Kane yanked his leg away from hers—"let me be."

Rowan felt like she'd just been punched in the gut. It took her a few seconds to recover enough to smile politely at the waitress who was asking for their appetizer order. Rowan blinked hard, hating herself for being this weak. For getting emotional over Kane pushing her away. This is what he did. This is how he'd made it so long without connecting with people. He'd trained himself to rip away if things got too deep, too serious. If someone got too close, he turned to embers and burned them for trying.

She swallowed hard, averting her gaze. "I should get to Harper's Mountains before they worry." Rowan stood and held out her hand for a shake. "It was nice to meet you, Kane."

He sat there shaking his head, arms crossed, jaw clenched, red creeping up his neck. She didn't know why he was refusing to look at her, but she finally gave up and dropped her hand to her side, then made her way down the stairs and back to her car. She forced herself not to look back because she didn't want him to see the tears streaking her make-up.

Let me be.

Fine. If he wanted her to treat him like everyone

else, that was his choice. It wasn't hers. If it was up to her, she would become his best friend and make him crave her touch, make him want her kisses, but Kane wasn't like her. And she had no right to shove him into a box. He liked his life and made it abundantly clear that he didn't want friends. That he didn't want her.

And as she pulled out of the parking lot, it hit again—The Sickening. Blood trickled down her lip and made the air smell like copper, but luckily, this one wasn't so bad. Just a few drops, and it was done.

She would go deep into Harper's Mountains and set up a temporary home, hug her friends, and in three tiny days, she would have her treasure again. Kane could go back to his life, and everything would be okay for the both of them separately.

Except the farther she drove away from Kane, the more her chest hurt. She wasn't good at see-ya-laters, and she might never see the Blackwing Dragon again.

It should've been a relief since she wasn't supposed to be friends with the enemy.

But it wasn't.

Leaving Kane physically hurt.

EIGHT

Rowan leaned forward and squinted at the sign on the side of the road. At some point it had read *Boiled Peanuts*, but someone had spray painted a thin layer of white over the B and the Pea, and now it read *oiled nuts*. There was also a hideous painting of an owl with a giant pecker in the bottom corner. Looked like Ryder had struck this place hard. He'd used the same ugly tag when he'd vandalized water towers, street signs, and Willa's Wormshack when they were kids.

Shaking her head, she took a right onto a dirt road as the rented GPS told her to do. For the tenth time on the drive into Nantahala, she was stunned by the scenery. Everything was so lush and green, like a jungle. A river wound right by the road on one side, and on the other, a mountain went straight up to the sky. Vines hung down from tree branches so low they almost touched her convertible, and the chirping of bugs was a constant song outside as she cruised with the top down.

Harper's Mountains were so different from Damon's Mountains.

About thirty-seven potholes later, she reached an open gate. The car bumping and bouncing, she slowed in front of a small cabin with some familiar forest green shutters. Weston must've taken them from the old trailer, 1010, and put them on this place. It was late afternoon, but it looked like evening here on account of the mountains and thick forest canopy blocking out the sunlight. Up the dirt road were more rustic cabins, but Rowan stopped in front of the first one with the shutters.

She got out and hesitated on the bottom stair. The number beside the door was crooked, but easily readable. 1010. Gooseflesh blasted up her arms.

An ear-splitting whistle made her hunch her shoulders and cover her ears. Ryder was trotting down the road toward her, followed by a dark-haired woman with a big, greeting smile on her face.

Weston came out of a cabin up the road, and farther up, Aaron, Harper, and Wyatt were running beside a couple of women Rowan didn't recognize.

She bolted for Ryder, the closest, and he caught her midair, crushed her to him and spun her around, clapping her on the back and laughing. "Holy fuck, scaredy dragon, you came out of Damon's Mountains."

"Hey, I came out a couple weeks ago for Weston."

"Because Beaston made you. This one is voluntary."

Rowan thought about how Damon and Weston had bullied her into coming here, but okay. She would let Ryder think her a heroine for a little while longer. Rowan was all giggles as she wiggled out of Ryder's arms and reached for Weston, then Aaron. She met Ryder's mate, Lexi, and shook her hand, then Alana, Aaron's mate, who was quite possibly the most striking woman she'd ever laid eyes on. Curvy, beautiful dark skin, bright gold eyes like Aaron's, and a beaming white smile that made a scar from lip to her nose even deeper.

Avery, Weston's mate, was quiet and had trouble

meeting her eyes, but she gave Rowan a hug and said, "Thank you for coming to help us at Raven's Hollow." Was she crying? Rowan gave her another hug, a tighter one, a longer one because it must've been very scary for a timid raven shifter to go against her people. Rowan remembered her. Avery had fought fiercely beside Weston while Rowan had been terrified just to leave Damon's Mountains. This little raven didn't know it, but she was braver than a dragon.

And then there was Wyatt, all spiked-up brown hair, piercing blue eyes, and that shit-eating grin that was just the same as when they were kids. Rowan was crying now, too, because Wyatt had disappeared at age eighteen, and she hadn't seen much of him since. Damn, it was good to hug him. He squeezed her tight, rocked them back and forth while she leaked tears onto his T-shirt.

"You were so angry when you left. So…"

"Shhhh," he said against the side of her head. He was stroking her hair like she was a babe in need of soothing. God, this felt good. "I'm okay now, Roe. Harper saved me."

A sob worked its way up her throat as she

reached for Harper with her other arm and hugged them both close. "You did good, Harper girl," she whispered.

Harper was sniffling, and now Rowan could feel hands on her back. She could feel the crew crowding close, touching her just to reassure themselves that she was here and she was all right. It was just like with the Gray Backs.

This should've been such a happy moment, but all Rowan could think about was Kane, sitting alone at the restaurant at the end of a bar, eating by himself. He would never have this because he would never allow it.

There was something so tragic about that.

Shaking her head to rid herself of thoughts that hurt her heart, Rowan eased back and cupped the tiny swell of Harper's belly. The Bloodrunners went quiet.

"Have you felt him kick yet?" she asked reverently. Harper was carrying the next generation Bloodrunner Dragon. She was carrying a little boy who would grow up mighty and fierce. A fire breather if Beaston's predictions were right, and they were always right.

Harper pressed her hands over Rowan's and shook her head. "Not yet. I've been drinking orange juice and lying on my back, but I think it's still too early. Rowan?"

Rowan looked up into Harper's eyes—one glowing blue with a long pupil, one soft brown. "Yeah?"

"Thanks for coming to protect my crew. It means…" Harper's eyes were rimmed with moisture, and she swallowed over and over again before she finished her thought. "It means the world to me. I know how hard it was leaving Damon's Mountains."

"Yeah, well," Rowan said shakily, "I couldn't leave the protection of the next Bloodrunner Dragon up to a bunch of wussy flight shifters."

"I resemble that," Ryder said, shoving her in the shoulder.

"It's *resent*," Weston said with a sigh, but his lips were curved up in a smile, and his green eyes, so much like Beaston's, were dancing with happiness. Whatever Avery was doing for Weston, Rowan liked her all the more for it. She'd never seen him give smiles this easily.

They all started walking toward the cabin, 1010,

and Aaron pulled her against his side, nearly squished the life from her, and ruffed up her hair. "I'll have you know we would've been fine without you. Bear is extra aggressive lately with Alana to protect and now Harper's pregnancy. I could've handled it all on my own."

"Okay, man," Wyatt said with an eye roll. "I could've offered a little help, too."

"And me," Alana said. "My bear is big and scary."

Aaron snorted. "Two days ago you asked me to paint your bear's claws pink with glitter."

"For science!" Alana exclaimed as the others laughed. "I wanted to know if my claws were painted, would my nails stay painted when I Changed back to my human form."

"Wait," Avery said. "Does it work like that?"

"That's why I asked him to do it, but he refused."

"Bad mate," Ryder said. "I would paint Lexi's if she asked."

"Mmm hmm," Lexi said, not falling for his bullshit. "And what would you have asked in return."

"Barbecue."

"And?" Lexi asked.

"Dick kisses," Ryder muttered.

Rowan bellowed a single, surprised laugh. "Alana, I'll paint your claws next time you Change. I've got you."

"Mmm, I like Rowan already," Alana said through a grin.

Rowan inhaled deeply as she listened to the chatter and laughter of the Bloodrunners. Things were different with her childhood friends now. They'd grown, settled down, bonded, and had all become closer without her. They'd become a family.

Everyone had moved on, and like Peter Pan, Rowan had stayed behind in Neverland.

She'd pitied Kane for clinging to his safe, lonely existence, but she had no right to.

Because she'd done the same thing.

NINE

Kane lifted the last three bags of dirt out of the back of his Bronco and made his way inside Martin's River Gem Mine. He worked here six days a week to cover bills and drinking money. He dumped the bags into the metal bin against the back wall of the shop and then made his way back around the racks of T-shirts and tables of crystals for sale. There was one last family under the metal awning outside, mining still, sifting through the dirt Kane and Wyatt had hauled down from the mountain.

Martin, the owner, was inside his office crunching numbers, like he always did at the end of a day, and Wyatt was outside, helping the clients identify gems they found.

Kane approached slowly, still unsure if he even wanted to open this can of worms.

He'd felt fucking sick for three days, just empty. He'd been hungry for something he couldn't identify, eaten meal after meal and never been sated. He was hollow. There had been no sleep thanks to the angel face that kept slipping across his consciousness. Blond hair, lighter at the ends, blue eyes, pixie lips, pert nose, little freckles, dark lashes. Those long legs and those hourglass curves, and fuck, he had to stop thinking about Rowan like this. He'd already beat off twice since last night. Why did his body crave her so damn bad? This wasn't like him. He fucked a woman every once in a while, and it tided him over. But this? He was obsessing. And it wasn't just in his mind either. His body was obsessing about her.

He'd hurt her. Fucking surprise, surprise. Kane hurting others was the most natural thing in the world. He hated it. Hated what he'd become. Hated the look of heartbreak he'd seen in her pretty eyes when he'd told her to leave him alone. She wore every emotion right there on her face for him to see. He could've stabbed her and got the same expression of pain. Rowan was too fragile for a man like him, so why was he so enthralled with her?

If he was a good and decent man, he would leave her alone. He would let her find someone who was a better match, but instead, he'd been thinking of ways to see her. Thinking of ways to run in to her.

He'd attached to a girl like this before, and she'd been Turned into a bear against her will.

He'd been this attached before, and he'd done something awful on her behalf.

He'd been this attached before, and it had ruined his entire life.

Rowan Barnett scared the shit out him.

And yet…

Here he was, considering talking to Wyatt. He was actually considering asking advice from another person who didn't owe him anything.

Wyatt looked up, nodded a greeting as he continued to talk to the clients about how rubies were cut. Fuck, he couldn't do this.

Kane did an about-face, which hurt his bad leg, but it was worth it if he could escape. He was a loner for a reason, and Wyatt accepted that about him. Best not to mess that up.

But Wyatt was a link to Rowan, and with every

step he made away, the emptiness yawned wider inside of him.

With a growl, Kane turned around again and forced himself straight to Wyatt, who was wearing the deepest frown Kane had ever seen on him. He looked wary, his eyes narrowed to little suspicious slits. Wyatt waved off the family, and Kane gave them a polite smile as they passed, chattering happily as they studied the rocks in their palms.

"Where are your sunglasses?" Wyatt asked.

"Oh, shit," Kane muttered, patting his pockets, checking the neck of his shirt. "I think I forgot them in my truck."

Wyatt sat on the bench by a trough of dirt and cocked his head. "What's wrong with you? You smell sick."

"I'm not sick, asshole. I'm just…" Sick. Kane cleared his throat. "I've never done this before."

"Forgot your sunglasses? No shit. I think I've seen your eyes like five times in the last three years. You look like a monster, man."

"Thanks." Kane wiped his sweaty palms on his jeans and gave his gaze to the woods behind Wyatt, to the ceiling of the shelter, to the troughs of dirt, to anywhere but Wyatt. "So, I was wondering if I could ask for some advice?"

Wyatt's eyebrows lifted nearly to his hairline. "You want to ask me for advice? Okay. Shoot."

"No, I mean. Maybe over drinks, or dinner. I can pay."

"Are you asking me on a date?"

"Fuck, Wyatt, give me a break, man. I don't know how to do this shit. What do guys do when they have girl problems? Shoot darts? Shoot whiskey? Whatever it is, I want to do that. Kind of."

"Wait, wait, wait, you have girl problems?" Wyatt's grin stretched across his whole face, and his blue eyes sparked with triumph. "This is awesome."

"Forget it," Kane muttered, heading for his Bronco.

But there was Wyatt, keeping pace with him. "Ryder calls these bro-dates."

"Well, we aren't bros, so…"

"You're driving. My truck is low on gas."

Kane cast him a quick glance to make sure Wyatt wasn't dicking him around, but he seemed serious enough when he said, "I'm gonna say bye to Martin. Meet you in the truck."

"Okay," Kane said, shocked that this was working. He thought Wyatt would've told him to fuck off immediately. He had the Bloodrunners after all, and Harper. His friend card was nice and full, and Wyatt and Kane hadn't exactly gotten along all these years. More like tolerated each other for work's sake.

Two minutes later, Wyatt was sitting in his passenger's seat, slamming the door closed beside him. As Kane pulled out of the gravel parking lot, Wyatt went to work poking buttons on his phone.

"What are you doing?" Kane asked suspiciously.

"Texting Ryder that you asked me on a bro date. He's gonna be so jealous."

"What? Why?"

"Because he's convinced you are his fourth best friend, and he's been waiting for you to call him to hang out."

Kane snorted. "Your entire crew is weird."

"Truth," Wyatt said easily, shoving his phone into his back pocket and resting his elbow on the open window. "Who is the girl?"

"Someone way too good for me?"

Wyatt huffed a breath. "Ain't that the way it works. She'll make you into a better man, though."

"Is that what happened with Harper?"

"Yessir. I had to up my game to keep her."

Kane cleared his throat again uncomfortably. "Sooo…what's it like being paired up with a dominant female? Dragon. I mean since you're a bear. Do you ever have trouble with the fact that she is alpha? That she's more dominant than you?"

"Nah. It's not like that. It's not like you think. Harper's dragon is badass, don't get me wrong, and if I piss her off, whoo, she can rage. But Harper the woman? She's kind and understanding. She's sweet and wants to do the right thing. She never makes me feel less than just because my animal is smaller. It doesn't come up, and being with her, it's worth the occasional moment of weakness on my part. It's worth the dark moments when I question if I'm good enough for her. That's up to me, to rise up and be good enough after everything, you know?"

Kane swallowed hard and nodded. Made sense. But at least Wyatt was a shifter. Kane's heart was chasing the biggest dragon shifter in the world, and he was nothing more than a man. He was a hundred levels below Rowan. He would never be able to protect her.

"I've never seen you show favor to a woman," Wyatt said quietly. "I've seen you be kind and respectful to the girls in my crew, but I've never seen you take anyone out on a date. Maybe you do, I don't know. I don't see you much outside of work, but you've never mentioned a woman before. This one must be big."

"She feels big." Kane ran his hand through his hair and pulled into the River's End, a bar and restaurant near an outdoor center advertising guided rafting and zip lining tours for tourists. It was usually busy as hell this time of day, but they could sit at the bar.

"Big how?" Wyatt asked as Kane shoved the Bronco into park.

"Scary."

"Shit, man. Sounds like you're in trouble with this one."

"Yeah."

He and Wyatt found a couple seats up at the bar, ordered a pair of jack and cokes and trout cakes over grits. The restaurant was right over the water, and a few straggling white water rafting tours were lazily floating by. Evening was casting the valley in shadows, but the warm glow of the restaurant settled the uncomfortable humming feeling in his chest. Or maybe it was Wyatt somehow. Just talking about Rowan made him feel better. Or maybe it was the shiny rock he was turning over and over in his hand while he waited for his drink to arrive.

"What's that?" Wyatt asked, jerking his chin at the stone.

"The girl gave it to me. Said she was giving me a treasure."

"So she knows what you are?"

Kane snorted and leaned forward on his elbows. "She knows what I'm supposed to be. You and I both know I'm just a man."

"Just a man with dragon eyes and the strength of a shifter. They didn't cut him out of you completely, Kane."

Kane shook his head. "I don't want to talk about that shit, man."

"Well, maybe you should. Ain't no shame in what happened to you."

Other than Rowan, Wyatt was the only one who knew his dragon was inaccessible. He'd found out by accident.

"I heard what happened with Ryder's dad."

When the bartender set a drink in front of him, Kane downed it neatly and gestured for another. He needed to have a buzz for this conversation. "I wanted to kill him."

"Understandable."

"Is it?" Kane arched his eyebrows at Wyatt. "Is it understandable that I don't even have the dragon, and I still have such a darkness inside of me that I would've killed that man, no remorse, if Ryder and Weston weren't there to stop me? Nah. You're a shifter, Wyatt."

"So?"

"So you view death differently than normal people. You see the necessity in killing because it's your nature. Because it's how you grew up, with shifter wars and fights to the death. I didn't grow up like that. I grew up with humans, and they don't see the necessity in killing, not even if the person is evil, not even if it's to save your life. If they find out you're a killer, they shun you, shackle you, and rip the dark from you."

"They failed with you though, Kane," Wyatt said low. "You're still here. A woman could make things easier."

He huffed a breath and downed the second drink the bartender put in front of him. "Another please." Kane leveled Wyatt with a hard look. "If you were me and cared about a woman, would you strap her with the shit I shoulder?"

Wyatt sighed and crossed his arms. "Does she like you back?"

"I don't know. Felt like it when we kissed, and she's affectionate with me, but I don't know for sure. She could just be like that, you know?"

"So what you just told me is she does know about the dragon, about the shit that happened, about your eyes, about the extra shifter shit you have, and she still kisses you. She still touches you. So she's not afraid of you?"

Kane thought of what Rowan's fire-breathing, badass dragon must look like. "No man. She has no reason to be."

"Then I'd say she likes you fine, and it should be her decision whether she wants to shoulder your baggage with you. I was like you—"

"I doubt it—"

"We're more alike than you think, Kane. That pit

inside of you that doesn't ever get filled? I had one of my own for a long time. Harper and I lost a baby when we were eighteen. It ripped me up, ripped her up."

"A baby could've killed her," Kane murmured, confused.

"Yeah, but she wanted Janey. She wanted her so bad, and I just wanted Harper to live. I didn't want to be the one who killed her. And she lost that little baby, and there was this moment of relief, like I'd chosen Harper's life over Janey's, and I felt awful for it. I spiraled. I left Damon's mountains, left Harper when she needed me. I lost myself and got so fucking dark I couldn't see any light anymore."

"How did you dig out?"

"I didn't. Harper dug me out. She gave me this little ray of light to get me going again. She gave me hope, and I got my hands moving. I got to work so I could see more light, and there she was, standing there, arms open even though I didn't deserve it. I'm telling you, man. Just because it's dark right now, that don't mean it always has to be that way."

"So you think I should go after this woman?"

"Yeah, Kane. If she feels scary to you, I'd say

that's a good sign. I know you're careful about opening up, but you never know what can happen. You just don't until you give someone that chance to let you down or love you."

Love. That was a big, terrifying word. Rowan wouldn't be able to do that. Not with him. Not when she found out all the awful stuff about him. But God, did it sound tempting to try for something like Wyatt had with Harper and Ryder had with Lexi. Like Weston had with Avery and Aaron had with Alana.

Kane lowered his voice and pulled the new drink the bartender gave him closer. "I heard about Harper."

Wyatt froze. "What about her?" he asked carefully.

Kane tinked his glass gently against Wyatt's. "Congrats man. I'm happy for you. I hope…"

"Harper is strong enough," Wyatt said firmly. "She'll get him to air, and she'll survive it." But it sounded as though he was trying to convince himself as much as Kane.

"He'll be a brawny little titan," Kane said. "You'll be good at this father crap."

Wyatt chuckled and relaxed, downed his drink

with Kane. "God, I hope so. I'm about to be a lone grizzly shifter in a family of dragons. I'm about to be outnumbered by the fire-breathers, man."

"Nah, you have the crew. They say it takes a village to raise a child. You've got the village, Wyatt, and between you and your mate, your boy will be lucky." Lord knows Kane could've used a village like that growing up.

A loud rumbling sounded down the road, and Wyatt turned, glanced over his shoulder at the wall of windows. "Speaking of the village."

Dread dumped into Kane's system when he looked behind him. One Bloodrunner he could handle. The whole crew he needed to mentally prepare for. He stood up too quickly, and his stool scooted loudly across the wooden floor.

Wyatt's hand was on his arm in an instant. "Nope, sit down. Ryder won't let you get away, might as well hang out for half an hour before you duck out."

He didn't want to do this. Being around such a close-knit group always reminded him of what he didn't have. It always made him recognize what a fucking outsider he was. But as he moved to pull his wallet from his back pocket to pay, a familiar set of long legs stepped from the back door of a jacked-up, charcoal gray pickup truck.

Kane's heart hammered against his sternum. He froze like a dope, completely entranced with Rowan's graceful stride. She wore a loose, see-through knit sweater that hung off her shoulders over cut-off jean shorts and flip flops. Her hair was pulled in a high ponytail that trailed blond tresses down her long neck and swished from side to side as she walked toward the restaurant talking with Alana.

And there was no leaving now. There was no more avoiding the apology she deserved.

There was no more avoiding the girl who had taken up all his headspace for three straight days.

Sounds like you're in trouble with this one.

Wyatt didn't even know how right he'd been.

TEN

"It's early mornings, though," Alana warned about the job she'd just offered Rowan. "Early mornings, but then we close up around two or three in the afternoon, so you get a good chunk of the day off."

"It sounds perfect. I don't mind the hours at all," Rowan said excitedly. Honestly, she'd expected a real hard time finding a job since she was a dangerous shifter, but Alana had just offered out of the blue on the drive over here.

Rowan couldn't stop smiling. Her cheeks were actually getting tired right now! She pressed her palms to her cheeks to cover the blush there and turned to Alana in front of the River's Edge restaurant Ryder insisted they go to. "Alana, this means more than I can even tell you. I'll be the best employee you ever had. I swear you won't regret this."

Alana pulled her hands away from her face and grinned. "You can start on Wednesday. I'll get you an apron with the logo, a nametag, and everything. Training starts at six."

Rowan made a high-pitched squeal and hugged Alana's shoulders tight. Must've been too tight because Alana grunted a pained sound, and Aaron snarled from behind her. "Oops, sorry." She released Alana and put some space between her and Aaron. She loved him like a brother, but Bear had always been a beast. Aaron's eyes were bright gold right now, and he stank of dominance. Second in the crew had made his animal even heavier than she remembered. Probably having a mate to defend now didn't help.

Alana squeezed her hand in silent forgiveness, and then she wrapped her arms around Aaron's waist. He was even bigger than she remembered, tall and blond like a Viking, tattoos everywhere, broad-shouldered, and those eyes... Aaron had grown up to be a warrior.

Rowan watched them make their way inside and swallowed hard. She was brought here to protect the Bloodrunners. To protect badass shifters like Aaron? Like Wyatt and Alana? Like two of the most battle proven flight shifters in the world—Weston and Air Ryder? She was in way over her head. God, she hoped there was zero trouble so Rowan wouldn't fail the Bloodrunners.

It was getting dark out, but River's Edge was a long cabin set right beside the river. The soft, inviting glow of artificial light streaming through the numerous windows beckoned to her. Movement caught her attention, and she locked eyes on a man she thought she would never see again. Kane. He was wearing a thin black T-shirt that clung to his chest and shoulders, and his tattoos down one arm were stark against his pale skin. His hair was tossed to one side and fell forward in front of the left side of his face in dark waves. She hadn't noticed how big he was until now when he was surrounded by humans. He was a full head taller and much wider than any of them. He stood as frozen as her, trapping her with that inhuman gaze. And thank God for tiny blessings—he wasn't wearing those damn sunglasses tonight.

He was stunning.

He'd also told her to leave him alone. Was he angry she was here? She couldn't read the expression on his face. It wasn't her fault. Ryder had said Wyatt was out drinking and told her to get dressed, end of story.

Rowan swallowed hard and lifted her fingers in the air, gave him a little wave.

Kane leaned over to Wyatt at the bar, murmured something, then strode toward her. Shit, he was coming. Rowan tugged at the hem of her shirt and rushed to make sure it was settled on her shoulders just right. She pulled her ponytail tighter and pursed her lips, checking on the consistency of her lip gloss. *Be cool.*

Rowan cocked her hip and crossed her arms, then felt stupid so she let her hands drop down to her sides as he came out the swinging door.

"Hey—"

"Hidey ho—" she said at the same time he greeted her.

Rowan laughed nervously. Kane ran his hand

through his hair, smoothing it out of his face as he tracked a slow moving car behind her with his gaze. "So, I fucked up the other day. I popped off because I didn't like where the conversation was going, and I handled it all wrong."

"Oh." Rowan looked at her painted pink toes. "If you could go back, how would you do it differently?"

A smile ghosted his lips. "I would've gone after you. I would've caught you before you got in your car and drove away. I would've said sorry then and let you leave on a better note."

Rowan was trying her best to hide a smile. He shouldn't be off the hook this easily, but something inside of her said Kane didn't apologize often. "Is that all?"

Kane scrubbed his hand down his dark facial scruff and stepped closer. He brushed her hip with his finger and looked uncertain as hell. He lowered his voice to a deep rich timber that lifted the fine hairs on her body. "I maybe would've got your phone number too. I'm sorry, Roe. I didn't mean what I said. I don't want you to let me be."

"Oh, so you want me to continue annoying the shit out of you?"

Kane snorted. "Apparently."

She shoved him in the chest, but he didn't move or flinch away from her. He laughed instead. God, she loved the way laughter sounded from him, so easy and deep. He caught her hands, intertwined their fingers, leaned forward like he was going to kiss her.

Knock, knock, knock! A fist pounded on the glass window of the restaurant, and Ryder's muffled voice carried through. "Gross, are you two gonna make out?"

Kane froze like an ice sculpture, then eased away and looked back over his shoulder. In the River's Edge, all the Bloodrunners were staring at them through the window, expressions of utter shock eerily similar on all their faces. Ryder's mouth was hanging open, and his hands were smushed against the glass.

Kane muttered his favorite word. His body hummed with stress, so Rowan wrapped her arms around his waist and rested her chin between his defined pecs, stared up into his eyes.

Kane stumbled backward a step and righted his balance. He dragged in a long, ragged breath and murmured, "Princess, it's terrifying how easily you make me lose my head."

That didn't sound like such a bad thing, though.

Rowan pulled his hand toward the restaurant, but Kane balked outside the door. "Wait, wait, wait."

"What's wrong?"

"I just need a minute."

Rowan looked from him to the Bloodrunners through the window, who were dispersing and meandering toward a bar area. "Do you not like them?"

"No, no, it's not that. It's just…I'm not good in crowds."

"In crowds of shifters?"

"Yeah, that."

"Who do you like best?"

"What?"

"Out of the Bloodrunners, who do you get along with best? Who do you connect with most?"

"Besides you?"

Rowan ginned, flattered. "Yeah, besides me."

"Wyatt is okay. Avery, too. She's calm and quiet."

"Good. Okay. Kane," she said, cupping his cheeks and pulling his troubled gaze from the window. "I'm really hungry. I haven't eaten since breakfast, and I feel weak."

Kane was nodding, and his elongated pupils dilated. "I should feed you."

She bit her lip hard to hide her smile. Kane was just like every other dominant male shifter she knew. He might think himself only a man, but he was wrong. His dragon had more sway than he realized. The urge to protect and take care of a female's needs was just as strong in Kane as it was in the Bloodrunner men inside.

"I want to eat with you, and I'll be right there, pestering you all night, so you don't have to worry about anyone else, okay? Just me."

"Yeah," Kane rumbled.

He opened the door for her and pressed his fingertips on her lower back, guiding her inside. She didn't miss it, though. His hand was shaking. Her protective instincts reared up like the monster from the depths of Loch Ness.

Rowan led Kane to the bar and positioned him right between her and Avery, who gave him an immediate hug. His shoulders were tensed up hard, but he patted her on the back awkwardly and tried to smile. Wyatt gave him the strangest look, flashed the same look to Rowan, then handed Kane a drink and shoved a plate of what looked like trout and grits down the bartop to him. But Kane didn't dig in, no. He ushered Rowan onto the bar stool and gestured for her to eat up. Then he turned, the tension easing from his body, and got pulled straight into a weird hug from Ryder—one where Ryder rested his head against Kane's chest and gave Rowan a mushy smile. "You two will make beautiful dragon babies."

"Jesus," Kane muttered, clapping him once on the back. "That's good, man."

Ryder held on. "I predict a dozen fire-breathers."

Kane was looking up at the ceiling now with his hands out. Since his lips were moving, Rowan was pretty sure he was counting to ten for patience. She snickered and scarfed another bite.

Ryder eased back, and Kane's clenched jaw relaxed, up until the point Ryder pulled his phone up and took a quick selfie of them and began typing away. "Hashtag fourth best friend. Hashtag Dark Kane," Ryder murmured.

"I don't want to be on your social media, Ryder," Kane said low.

Ryder snorted. "It's not mine. I'm adding our

picture to your account."

Kane's eyes narrowed to suspicious green slits. "I don't have an account."

"Yeah, you do. I made it for you. You have two thousand followers. Two-thousand and one. Two-thousand and six. Ha! Look." Ryder turned his phone toward Kane and showed him the climbing number of followers. The profile pic was one Ryder had obviously taken while Kane wasn't paying attention. It featured Ryder's smiling face and Kane sitting a few chairs down the bar with his sunglasses on, watching a television, completely unaware.

Rowan pursed her lips so she wouldn't laugh as hard as she wanted to. "Friend-request me," she told Ryder, then winked at Kane and said, "We're besties."

Kane looked so defeated.

The food was freaking delicious, so she shoved a bite at him. He looked taken aback completely. "Are we sharing?"

Ryder, still staring at his phone, said, "You almost sucked face with her outside, man. Methinks you should worry less about Roe's cooties."

Kane took the bite quick, then gestured to a passing bartender and ordered another plate of trout and grits and a couple shots of whisky.

"I hope those are both for you," Rowan teased, then told the bartender she wanted, "A panty-dropper drink. Something pink and fruity." Kane groaned behind her, but he would have to get used to her tastes.

"Tonight, I'm celebrating." She fed him another bite, and he didn't even balk this time.

"Yeah? What are you celebrating?"

"Alana just offered me a job at her coffee shop. I don't even have to job hunt!"

Kane's eyebrows winged up, and he cast a stunned look at a grinning Alana. "Really?"

"I have a good feeling about her," Alana said, lifting the straw of her Sex on the Beach to her lips. She took a long draw and then said, "She starts next week. Gonna make sure she gets her treasure back before she starts work."

Kane jerked his attention back to Rowan. "You don't have it yet?" He smelled worried.

"It's supposed to be delivered to Harper's Mountains any time now. Hopefully tomorrow is the day. They found it. The suitcase is just in transit."

Kane opened his mouth to say something, but

the bartender handed him drinks. "Thanks," Kane murmured, then squared up to Rowan, right between her legs, looking down at her with those fiery green eyes. Voice pitched low and gravelly, he asked, "Have you been sick?"

Rowan sighed because she didn't want to think about it. She wanted a night to escape the stress of the last few days and not dwell on how freaking terrified she was. "Yes."

"Roe," Kane whispered.

She forced a chipper smile and bunched the waist of his T-shirt in her clenched fists. "I feel good tonight, though." Determined to distract him, she handed him one of the shots of whiskey and held up the other. She cocked her eyebrow in a dare.

Kane angled his head, his eyes tightening in the corners, but he gave in and bumped his tiny glass against hers. They both clinked the bottoms of their shot glasses against the counter gently, then threw back the burning liquid.

Tasted like piss, so Rowan chased it with a few desperate slurps of Avery's ice water. She coughed while Kane laughed at her.

"Stop," she complained, shoving him. The brute

didn't even move. That was something she was still trying to get used to. That kind of force with anyone else, and they would've gone flying.

Kane made no sense. No dragon, which she had a million questions about, and slowed healing, but he still had dragon eyes and brute strength.

"Why don't you use your dragon?" she asked, feeling the buzz.

"Nope," he clipped out, then leaned way over her and took a bite of their food.

"Fine, what were you doing around Saratoga?"

He frowned. Around the bite, he asked, "What do you mean?"

"On the plane, you happened to be at the same place as me. But you talk about Damon like you're scared of him, so why were you in his territory, mysterious dragon?"

Kane growled a convincing sound and tried to retreat, but Rowan wrapped her arms and legs around him like a cat on a tree. "No use running. I'll chase you."

"I'm going to take a piss."

"Kane, I'm serious. I'll follow you."

He gave her a wicked grin. "Don't tempt me."

She thought about the women he'd fucked in bathrooms and wanted to kick both of his shins and maybe his chode, too. "You don't tempt *me*, Kane. I brought sanitary wipes in my purse."

He clipped out a surprised laugh and dragged his fingertips down her thighs. "Sanitary wipes?"

"Yeah, I'm not fucking in a germy bathroom."

Kane laughed a little harder and stopped struggling away from her grasp. "So, let me get this straight. You aren't opposed to fucking in a bathroom, but only if you wipe it down first?"

"If it erases those other women from your mind," she gritted out.

Kane smoothed his hair out of his face and looked around at the others like he was making sure they weren't listening. "Are you jealous of those girls? I never even saw them again."

Rowan crossed her arms over her chest and ducked his gaze. Why was she so angry right now? It was hard to even see straight. "I don't get jealous."

"Lie."

"Oh, you don't have a dragon, but you can hear lies?"

The smile dipped from Kane's lips. He

disconnected his touch from her, leaned his elbows on the bar, gave his attention to the television on the wall by the glass case of bourbon.

Remorse surged through her, chasing the fury out of her veins. "Hey," she whispered, rubbing her hand up his tensed back. "I'm sorry. I shouldn't keep bringing that up."

"You really shouldn't," Kane said, giving her a fiery look. His eyes looked even brighter now, but maybe it was the lighting. "It sucks to think about."

"Is that why you don't like hanging out with shifters?"

He huffed a humorless breath and forked a piece of fish, then pushed it around the plate like he'd lost his appetite. "Shifter or human, it doesn't matter. I don't belong with either."

And she could see his point. If he hung out with humans, he had to hide his eyes and his strength. It wasn't something they would ever get used to. If he hung out with shifters, he had to hear them talking about their animals openly, and he'd lost his somehow.

Kane was stuck between two worlds, all alone.

Rowan buried her face against his side and

hugged his waist tight. "You belong with me." She murmured it against his ribs so she wouldn't see the rejection in his eyes.

He didn't say anything back, but he did sigh and let his arm rest around her shoulders.

Kane left his arm there, allowed her to hug his side as he talked to the others. Little by little, he loosened up and started laughing and chatting with Wyatt, Ryder, and Aaron. The boys kept throwing her strange glances, but she didn't care if she was clinging to Kane like a rock oyster on an ocean boulder. She felt good touching him, and after the last few days of fear and uncertainty, she was holding on to this feeling of safety. She was going to cling to Kane as long as he allowed it.

The next hour passed in a blur of laughter and chaos as they ate and ordered drinks with the Bloodrunners. All but Harper, who was drinking water like it was going out of style. Little baby dragon sure made her thirsty lately.

Weston had been hanging back, cuddling Avery, but watching Rowan and Kane. She didn't miss it. His wary frown had drifted to them time and time again.

Weston made his way to Kane, then shook his

hand hard, pulled him in and clapped him on the back once. Rowan didn't like that he'd sidled between her and Kane to talk to him, but Avery was talking to her, asking what she'd done for work before she'd come to Harper's Mountains, and Rowan didn't want to be rude. She chatted with Avery readily enough, but her ears and her attention were focused on Weston. Mostly because he was being a doucheball.

"Man, it's not my place to say who you hang out with," he told Kane, "but I have to tell you, I don't like this." He lowered his voice. "Rowan's been through hell. She's finally out of Damon's Mountains, and I get this bad feeling you will chase her right back there."

"You're right, Wes," Kane said in a low rumble. He blinked slowly and leveled him a fierce look. "It's not your place."

"Yeah," Weston said, his voice turning rough and pissed. "Except I had this little dream of Rowan, and in it, she was surrounded by fire, and she was crying. And now it's making a lot of damn sense seeing you here with her. 'Scuse me if I want my friend to survive you, Dark Kane."

She didn't like that everyone called him Dark Kane, and a low rumble vibrated up Rowan's throat.

Dragon hated it, too.

"Not my fire," Kane said. "Rowan's safe from me."

"Doesn't feel like it, man."

"Weston," Rowan ground out. "That's enough."

"Did you tell him what happened yet?"

"Wes, stop."

"But Roe—"

"You want to get out of here?" she asked Kane quickly. She needed to get away from Weston and his annoying judgements. Away from him and his secrets he seemed so excited to expose, the dick.

"Yeah, let's go," Kane said, throwing down money for their food and drinks.

He stood to his full height and clapped Weston on the shoulder. He gave a lethal smile and said, "Don't worry, *Novak*. I'll get her home safely. You don't have to wait up."

Weston lurched forward but Wyatt was there, holding him back. "What the fuck is wrong with you, man?" Wyatt had a death grip on his shirt, shoving him backward, but Kane hadn't moved, as if welcoming another fight.

Rowan stood between them and urged Kane toward the door. "We'll talk about this later, Wes," she said through a disapproving frown.

"Rowan, I think you should go back home."

"And I think you should mind your own business," she snapped as Kane pulled from her grasp and walked away. "I don't need you to make decisions for me."

"And how many times did I save your ass in the Gray Backs?" he asked. "Huh? How many, Roe? How many times did I point out your bad decisions before you made them? How many times was I right?"

"I'm not that kid anymore, Wes! You've grown. You found a life outside of the mountains, away from me. You found a mate, and you found your place. Well, I grew up, too. Let me find my place now."

Weston shook his head and gritted his teeth. "Not with him, Roe. I have this awful feeling…I can't explain it. Just…don't pick Dark Kane."

"Stop calling him that." Rowan shook her head sadly, so disappointed in him. "You don't know him."

"I do."

"Not like I do. You're being an asshole, Wes. Rein it in."

She spun on her heel and strode for the door.

Wes was entitled to his opinion. Hell, all the

Bloodrunners were because they were her friends and allowed to worry. But she didn't have to listen to their advice, and especially not advice that was meant to sting.

Wes was wrong, and her instincts were different now.

Kane wasn't bad for her. He made her happy. He made her forget about her lost treasure and about the nosebleeds. He made her forget about her homesickness.

Anyone who made her this happy couldn't be bad for her.

ELEVEN

Kane was outside of the River's Edge, his sexy butt hanging out the passenger's side of his Bronco as he dug around for something.

"You okay?" she asked, wringing her hands. Tonight had been almost perfect, and then Weston had to go and get all big-brother-overprotective.

"I'm fine," Kane gritted out. He shoved off the seat and Rowan's heart dropped to the dirt parking lot when she saw what he'd found. His sunglasses were back in place.

"Kane, I don't want you hiding from me."

"I'm not hiding, Rowan. I shouldn't have taken them off in the first place. I think you should go back in there with your crew."

"They are my friends, Kane. Not my crew. I'm a Gray Back."

"And I'm nothing!" When Kane took a step back, his back hit the side of the Bronco so hard the truck rocked. "Fuck." Kane bit his lip and stared across the road at the ivy-covered mountain that protruded from the earth. "Wes is right."

"That's great, Kane."

"Roe, he saw fire, and he has a bad feeling about me—"

"You said you don't have the fire."

"But what if I somehow put you in danger? What if I bring on Damon's wrath, or piss off some other fire-breather we don't know about, or I don't know! My life isn't easy. I have people wanting to fight all the damn time, Rowan. I'm a rogue. Shifters and vamps can sense I'm weak. They just can't figure out why. So they fight. It's instinct. I'm a target, and Wes has some magic mojo shit that helps him see the future, and we should take it seriously. I'm not meant to be with someone. I'm not meant to be with you. I'll hurt you."

"You're being mean again."

"I'm not."

"You are. You say I'm a dragon and question why I'm afraid of everything, but then you sit here and tell me I should be afraid? That you're some threat to me? Have I ever called you Dark Kane?"

Kane ran the edge of his thumbnail over and over the scruff on his chin. He sighed an irritated breath and leveled her with a look.

Rowan repeated louder, "Have I?"

"No."

"Because you aren't Dark Kane to me. Push the world away all you want to, but it won't scare me off. It'll make me hold on tighter."

"Why?"

"Because I'm a dragon," she murmured. "We're a loyal bunch."

Kane crossed his arms, splayed his legs on the gravel, and leaned hard against his Bronco. "What did Wes mean in there? What happened to you? What did he protect you from?"

"Nope," she said, using his word to cut off the conversation.

"Roe."

Dang him using her friend name so she got all mushy and wanted to say yes to him. "Wes grew up with sisters, got all protective, and we were in the same crew, so he lumped me in with them. Thought he had to save me from every damn thing." She swallowed hard and kicked a rock. "Except some things he couldn't protect me from. I think he blames himself, but he takes it out on me."

"What do you mean?"

"I mean, he tried to stop something, and I messed up. He carries a lot of guilt over it. So he reminds me about the bad decision because that's how he is. He's angry I didn't listen to him, and to mask his own guilt over it happening, he gives me shit."

"Come on, princess," he murmured, limping past her.

"Where are we going?"

"I need to sober up before I drive you home, and I can't stand still when we talk like this. It makes me feel like I'm busting up inside. Let's go on a walk."

"Oh." She followed directly. "You know, for a second there, I thought you were gonna lead me around the side of the building."

Kane snorted and tossed her a look. "You really want me to fuck you in an alley?"

"It would be *so* romantic."

At least he was smiling again, so there was that. Rowan yanked the sunglasses off his face fast.

"Give them back," Kane said, reaching for them.

Rowan danced away and put them in her hair like a headband. "I'm about to confess my deepest darkest secrets to you, Blackwing. I'm not doing it while you hide from me."

"I already told you I'm not hiding."

"Bullshit, and you can do it with everyone else, fine. Not with me though. We're friends on social media now. It's getting serious."

Kane huffed an annoyed sound. "I'm deleting that account as soon as I get home."

"If I tell you why I got trapped in Damon's Mountains, will you tell me what happened to your dragon?"

"Nope." Kane cast her a quick, glowing-eyed glance, and then bumped her shoulder gently as they strode side by side over a wide bridge toward the outdoor excursion center. "I'll tell you someday, but not tonight. It's not something I've ever talked about, and I need to think on it first. It'll…it'll hurt to say it out loud."

"Hurt me or you?"

"Both, and I want you to like me for a little while longer. I like the way you look at me. Like I'm good."

Rowan slipped her hand into his and squeezed. "You are good."

Kane's smile was completely gone now, and he looked a little sick in the glowing lamp lights of the outdoor center. He shocked her to her bones by lifting her knuckles to his lips. They were soft against her skin, and hot like fire.

The night was quiet other than the wind in the rustling tree branches and the gentle rush of the river rapids below them. There was a bite in the air, and the soft hum of music from the River's Edge drifted to her on the breeze.

"My parents are really in love," she said as they stepped off the bridge and onto a stony bank of the river.

"That's good."

"My dad actually taught me how to swim instead of taking me to lessons like the other kids in my crew, and I remember my mom would watch our lessons with this proud smile on her face." Rowan kicked out of her flip flops and waded into the lapping shallows. "I grew up thinking her proud smile was for me. For how well I was catching on. But I overheard them one night, up late after I'd gone to bed, and my dad was talking to my mom about the night his mother drowned him in a bathtub."

"Jesus," Kane whispered. He kicked out of his shoes and socks, then waded in beside her.

"My dad barely survived, and from then on, he was terrified of water. He told her about how he'd tried to Change when his mom was drowning him, but he was so scared he couldn't call on his grizzly. And she succeeded. He blacked out. Died for a while maybe, I don't know, but she left him there floating in this deep claw foot bathtub while she turned off the lights and went to sleep like she hadn't just murdered her child. And I remember sitting in the hallway, knees drawn up to my chest, just…sobbing silently because I couldn't believe someone had done that to my daddy. And I couldn't believe he had gotten brave enough to learn to swim and then teach it to me. I also swore if anyone ever tried to do that to me, or to someone I love, I would never be too scared to Change. I made this pact with my dragon that we would protect each other and the ones we loved always. No matter what."

"How old were you?"

"Ten. Maybe eleven." Rowan puffed air out her cheeks and sat down on the clattering pebbles of the beach, her feet in the waves. Her butt was getting wet, but that was okay. Kane sat beside her, so close his arm brushed hers. So close she could feel his warmth, and it made her braver. "I fell in love with an older boy when I was really young. A kid still. Thirteen and he was sixteen. I had grown up watching my mom and dad, Willa and Matt, and Jason and Georgia. I'd watched Beaston and Aviana and their legendary love stories, and I was convinced I'd found my other half. His name was Byron and he lived down in Saratoga. Tall, mature, older, cute. He said all the right things, and I gave him my virginity way too early. Way too young, and it blinded me to the warning signs. I lived without regrets, convinced no one could ever fuck with me because I was a dragon. Wes saw lots of warning signs. He didn't like him, and neither did my parents, but that made me rebellious, you know? It made me like Byron more. He got me." She rolled her eyes at how stupid she'd been. "He asked a lot of questions about Damon. Too many questions, but we were in love and I didn't want to deny him, accuse him, or suspect him of anything bad. We had been dating for a few months when he asked me to catch a ride and meet him down at the library in Saratoga to study. I was grounded from him, my parents had even taken away my cell phone, and I was mad at the world. I thought they were just trying to keep my away from my true mate. But they were completely right, and I was completely wrong."

"What happened?"

"He and a five-man team kidnapped me, drugged me, and drove me six hours away from Damon's Mountains. I was in love with Byron, and he was ransoming me to Damon. I don't even think Byron was his real name, but I don't know what else to call him. I don't think he was really sixteen either, but just looked young."

"The police didn't find him."

A flash of fire blew across her mind, and her stomach curdled. "The police never caught wind of it."

"Did they…" Kane swallowed audibly gave his attention across the river. "Did they hurt you?"

"Not like that. They didn't want me for that

reason. It was for money, but I didn't know that at the time. They'd given me something to make me woozy. I remember flashes, you know? A dark room, handcuffs chaffing my wrists. A half empty water bottle. Them talking on the phone. Them putting the phone to my ear and telling me to, 'Say goodbye.' That was proof of life. I was shaking so bad and crying, then Damon's voice came over the line, 'Baby, are you all right?' But I wasn't. I wasn't okay. My dragon and I had broken our promise to each other. I was too scared to Change, and I knew exactly how my dad had felt when he was being drowned. I reached so hard, but I couldn't find her. My dragon was letting me down, I was letting her down, and something broke inside of me. The men wore ski masks in front of me, and they talked into the phone, told Damon they would kill me if he didn't follow their instructions and get them a ridiculous amount of money. Byron told me to scream, and when I spat at him, he hit me over and over. He wanted to scare Damon, but I held off. I wanted to be brave and keep the pain to myself so it wouldn't hurt my great grandfather, and eventually Byron switched tactics. He pulled out a knife and cut my hand. Cut it deep, and I gave him my voice. Another piece of me that he stole. I let him draw a scream from me, and I could hear Damon yelling across the phone, begging them to stop. He told me to Change and burn them to oblivion, and I couldn't. He called me Dragon, but she wasn't there, so I couldn't Change. I couldn't defend myself. I was shattering instead." She unclenched her fist and held her palm flat for Kane to see the silver, raised line on her skin.

He traced it with his fingertip, then brought it to his lips and lingered a kiss there. Rowan smiled, but the movement dislodged the two tears that had built up in her eyes. "The second day, the Gray Backs, the Ashe Crew, and the Boarlanders came for me. Damon came for me. Beaston had tracked me down, and I remember the roaring of the bears, then gunfire. Just...round after round, and I thought my people were getting hurt. I struggled against the handcuffs so hard, screaming for my dragon to come out of me so I could save them. Byron was guarding me, this automatic weapon trained at the door, but my dad, this massive pitch black grizzly, didn't use the door. He came barreling into the side of the cabin like a hurricane and ripped Byron limb from limb in front of me. It wasn't a clean kill, and I was horrified, just...so scared of what was happening. I kicked the pipe I was handcuffed to over and over until it busted. And then I ran out of the hole my dad had made. And all around was war. Guns and animals, and I stood in the middle of this killing field as Damon's blue dragon eclipsed the sun and blew fire at the men around me. He didn't know I was there. I could see the flames coming, and dragon's fire would kill me. Still, my dragon was quiet. My dad hit me from the side like a wrecking ball, and in an instant, we were under this old metal sign. You know the old thick ones that hang in vintage bars and country restaurants? My dad used it as a shield, but it wasn't big enough to cover him, and he was burned badly. Just a few seconds of blinding heat, and it was done. My dad was hurt because of me. I stared in horror as Damon devoured the ashes of my kidnappers." Rowan dared a glance at Kane as tears streaked down her cheeks. "Humans took me for money, and they shot at my people, they hurt my people, and it was my fault for trusting them."

"So you stayed in Damon's Mountains?"

She drew her knees up and rested her cheek on

them, nodded slowly.

"That's why you said you never felt safe enough to leave?"

Another nod because her throat was too tight after those mortifying admissions. "You got angry with me for wishing I was human, but my dragon got me taken, then she abandoned me when I needed her, and my people got hurt. My dad got hurt. A big part of me is still mad at her. A big part of me still doesn't trust her to come through for me if I ever need her like that again."

Kane pulled Rowan close and laid down, easing her down beside him. He held her tight against his side and pressed his lips against her forehead. Softly, barely loud enough to be heard over the breeze, Kane told her, "She'll come through for you, Bloodrunner. They drugged you, and they scared you, but they didn't break you."

He said it like he knew what it was to be broken, and it made Rowan want to cry harder. They were a mess, she and Kane. They were chaos and pain that somehow matched. "You know how you said you don't talk about your missing dragon with anyone?"

"Yeah," he said, staring at the stars above them

with a troubled set to his mouth.

"Well, I don't tell people about why I got stuck in Damon's Mountains."

"Ever?" he asked.

"Ever."

Kane laid his hand on his chest and inhaled deeply. "You know about genetic cleansing?"

Five words, but oh what they did to her. Rowan squeezed her eyes closed against the pain ripping through her chest. She'd wondered if that's what he had meant when he'd admitted he didn't have his dragon anymore, but she had hoped and prayed so hard that genetic cleansing wasn't a part of his story. "Yes," she whispered.

Kane's heart rate kicked up against her cheek. He hooked a finger under her chin and leaned down, pressed his lips against hers. It was gentle, but it was a lie. Kane wasn't in a gentle mood, evident from the rigidity of his body and that soft warning rumble in his throat as he eased away. He leaned in and placed his lips so close to her ear they brushed her sensitive lobe when he whispered, "That's what happened to my dragon."

TWELVE

Genetic cleansing.

For a moment, Rowan thought she would have to ask Kane to pull over so she could retch in the thick brush that lined the road.

She didn't know much about it, but what she did know, she'd avoided thinking about her whole life. It was unfathomable—the thought of someone systematically stripping an animal out of a shifter.

Kane took a right by an old, lopsided metal mailbox that was stuffed full of mail, as if he hadn't checked it in ages. He must not be checking it tonight either because he barely slowed for the turn onto the dark dirt road. He sped this way and that, expertly maneuvering his jacked-up Bronco around potholes she didn't even see until the last second. He probably knew every pit and rock in this area. Kane downshifted, then rested his hand on her knee. "Stop worrying, Rowan. It's over and done, and I've had half my lifetime to deal with this. It's okay."

"If it's okay, then why won't you tell me about it? Why won't you tell me what happened?"

Kane shook his head hard and turned up the music. Rowan turned the volume back to zero. "How long did it take?"

Another warning rumble filled the Bronco, and Kane grabbed the chest of his shirt and cut off the sound.

"How long?"

"A year for me. The Darkness didn't want to give up so it took twice the time."

Fuck. *Fuck*! He'd named his dragon The Darkness? And it took a year to kill him? *A year*?

Rowan wrapped her arms around her middle and leaned forward, hoping it would help the pain in her stomach. Kane pulled to a stop in front of an old, rundown cabin. It was surrounded by mountains and forest, but located right in the middle of a clearing. The shutters were barely hanging on, and the roof was rotten. Moss grew from the shingles, making the roof look green and squishy. The front porch sagged dangerously, and the stairs had rotted right through, but there was one nice wooden chair near the door. That was where Rowan threw her focus because, right now, it felt like the world was spinning out of control.

"How did they do it?"

"Roe, we aren't doing this. I'm not revisiting what was done. Please don't ask that of me."

Her face crumpled, and she held the back of her neck in her clammy hands just to cool herself down. "Was it that bad?"

Kane's profile was stony, and his eyes held ghosts as he stared at the house bathed in the headlights. He looked exhausted, as if the mention of genetic cleansing had siphoned all his strength from him. "It was fine."

Lie. It was a hollow lie. His voice gave him away.

Rowan wanted to cry for all he'd lost. She hated her dragon sometimes, wished she was human, but she hadn't thought about losing her dragon like this. She hadn't thought about the repercussions of someone actually ripping her animal away and killing it.

A year.

Rowan swallowed over and over, trying desperately not to get sick.

"Look, you should know why I brought you here," Kane rumbled low.

"Okay," she whispered.

"Two people have seen this place."

"Who?"

"Alana came by when I first moved to town. She brought me this welcome basket of local honey and grilling utensils, barbecue rubs, shit like that. It was the first time I met her. And Wyatt came over one night, uninvited. He was drunk as hell and had just had his neck ripped open by a vampire he used to feed. I think he was desperate to just connect with someone." Kane winced. "I'm not someone to connect with, though, so he never made it inside. I guess tonight…I guess I want someone to see me." Kane turned his face toward her and locked that inhuman gaze on hers. "Someone I trust."

Rowan glanced at a small black camera screwed to a tree out front, and another one on the front porch glinting off the headlights. Kane didn't trust much, but he was letting her in.

"You asked earlier what I was doing near Saratoga." Kane cut the engine and turned off the lights. He rested his head back against the seat and blew out a long breath. "I was visiting my mom and my brothers. My mom used to be scared of me, so I work hard to visit her and make sure she knows I love her. She'd been hurt by Marcus, and from day one, my dragon was a monster. A fire-breather that I had no control over. She didn't know how to raise me. Didn't know how to control The Darkness any more than I did. Right after my first Change, she moved us to a singlewide trailer close to Damon's Mountains. It was her way of bullying The Darkness into submission. The threat of Damon putting me down kept the dragon in better control. She had Damon on speed dial. She swore she would call him and have him kill The Darkness. That she would have him kill *me* if I became like Marcus, and I understood. I wasn't angry with her. I don't think Damon even knew we lived near his territory when I was younger, or if he did, he didn't ever show it. Didn't visit or call or chase us away. He just…let me exist, even as the son of his mortal enemy. Even as the last of Marcus's bloodline.

Every Change, I dreaded that he would show up and bring the dragon's fire that could kill me, but I didn't want to leave because in a way, The Darkness respected Damon. He behaved as well as he was able so he wouldn't draw the wrath of the blue dragon. Before you come inside my home, and before I share this part of myself with you, you should know something. You look at me and say I'm good, and you should understand before we go any further, that's not the case. The Bloodrunners have the right of it. You *should* call me Dark Kane. The Darkness was taken from me by order of the courts. There was no choice, Rowan. You have a black mark on your record, but I was so much worse than you. I'm a killer."

"Kane, war is different."

"I killed an eighteen-year-old civilian kid before I ever joined the army."

"Oh, my gosh."

"He was a shit. Turned this girl I cared about into a black bear against her will, and The Darkness took revenge."

Rowan frowned. Okay, that was different. That wasn't murder. That was justice. "Well, good."

Kane stared at her like she had two heads. "What?"

"Good, Kane. He would've been put down either way. That's against shifter law. If you Turn someone against their will, it's the alpha's job to put them down. No second chances."

Kane sat there frozen against his seat, staring at her with those flashing green eyes. Suddenly he sat forward and ran his hand down his face. "I'm sorry, what?"

"You carried out shifter law. Tough shit he was eighteen. Them's the rules. Humans don't get it, but they also don't live by the same laws we do."

Kane let off a huffed, humorless laugh. "You don't understand. I *killed* him."

"Because he killed that girl."

"Roe, stop it. You shouldn't just accept this and be okay with what I did."

"Where is the girl now, Kane?" She could guess, but Kane wasn't raised in a crew and obviously didn't know the consequences of a forced Turning. "What happened to her?"

Kane's Adam's apple dipped low in his muscular throat as he swallowed. His eyes flashed with disgust before he said, "Her black bear never came under her control. She ran away from home, became a meth addict, probably trying to stunt the bear. I tried to help as soon as I got out of the army, but she didn't want me to even look at her. Something was wrong with her. Something was broken by the time I got to her. She never registered with a crew, was ostracized from her family and her community, and five years ago, the police found her body, shotgun still in her hands."

Roe's heart physically hurt for the girl. "And what was her life before that boy took her humanity?"

Kane scratched the back of his head in irritation. "Straight-A student, popular, sweet, good family, good home, bright future. She was trying to get into Texas A&M University. It's all she'd wanted."

"When an animal is given to a human against their will, that animal is born into a body that hates it. It's born to chaos. Nine times out of ten, the animal will destroy the human from the inside out. You should let go of the guilt of killing that asshole, Kane. You did what was supposed to be done."

"Except it wasn't me who did the killing, Roe. It

was The Darkness. I wasn't even there. I was pushed out. I don't even remember what happened. Doesn't matter if it was the *right thing to do*. The Darkness didn't kill him out of some sense of heroic duty. He did it because he liked the kill."

"Bullshit."

"You don't know."

"I know better than you think! I have a dragon too, remember? I know how it is."

"You're a Bloodrunner."

"So?"

"So, you're good and light and your dragon has a moral compass. I'm the son of Marcus, Rowan. His flesh and blood *son*, conceived against my mother's will. The Darkness was an extension of him. I miss the dragon so fucking much I can't breathe sometimes. I miss flying. I miss breathing fire and eating ash. I dream of him. Dream of when my body made sense. Dream of when I wasn't empty. But my dragon wasn't a Bloodrunner like yours. He wasn't the good guy. The Darkness is in the grave where he belongs."

"Don't say that."

Kane made a frustrated ticking sound behind his teeth and shoved his door open, hopped out, and slammed the door behind him. She thought he was pissed at her, but he strode around the front and opened her door, averted his gaze, and held his hand out to help her down.

"Hey." Rowan cupped his cheeks, but he wouldn't look at her. She pushed on anyway because he should hear this. He should understand it. "The Darkness isn't dead, Kane. How can he be when you have his eyes? His strength? His voice?"

His lips twisted up in a cruel smile, and he jerked his head out of her hands. "These eyes are frozen into my face for a reason, Bloodrunner. They're the vacant, staring eyes of the animal that died inside of me. The Darkness isn't there anymore, Roe. I don't feel him anywhere. You can't save him. Can't resuscitate him. You have to be okay with this." Kane gestured to his body. "You get the shell or nothing at all."

She hated the way he said that. Kane wasn't a shell. He was warmth and understanding. He had been kind to her when she lost her treasure. He was complicated and real, and he made her heart beat faster in her chest when she was near him. He was good at his core but dangerous to anyone who threatened him. He was a beastly badass who didn't back down, but he turned gentle to her touch. He made her feel safe.

Silly man didn't see his worth like she did.

Dragon or no, he was the most interesting, seductive, alluring man she'd ever met. And now after hearing all that he'd survived—genetic cleansing, heavy guilt, war, and loss of his leg—he was also the strongest man she'd ever met. Here he was, still fighting, still surviving where others would've given up. He could've been like the girl Turned against her will who never came out of the tragedy, but Kane had locked his legs against the storm and absorbed blow after blow, became stronger for it, not beaten down.

He didn't realize it yet, but somewhere along the way, Kane had become the storm.

He'd become unbreakable, and a little terrifying.

Rowan was at the very beginning of her journey to find her strength, but Kane was already there. He had become stronger and harder until he was bulletproof. Until he had no urge to back down from a fight with anyone, anywhere. She'd seen it twice now—in the diner in Asheville and in the River's Edge tonight. She'd watched Kane's eyes go vacant and his lips twist into a wicked smile that said, *I fucking dare you to hit me*. Even without his dragon, Kane was a dominant, brawling beast of a man. He'd paused outside the door to gather himself, but didn't back down an inch when Weston came at him tonight. She loved that about him. She loved how complicated he was. How he could brush a light touch on her lower back, yet be so battle-ready in an instant.

Kane had fought for his life here, had been battling in the shadows for years, never complaining, never begging help, just surviving. The more she learned about him, the more he felt like hers. Like he was meant to be in her life. Meant to inspire her to be better, stronger, braver.

And her job in his? She was going to soften his heart just enough so that he would let her in. Kane was her match.

Sexy, dominant, lethal man with the power of a dragon.

Kane was watching her with that dangerous smile of his. The one where only the very corners of his lips curved up, and his eyes flashed with a shocking intensity that made her sex pulse between her thighs. His hair had fallen forward, and his fists were clenched, making his arm muscles bulge. As though he could feel the sexual charge that hung in the air between them, he dragged his hungry gaze slowly down her body, and wherever his attention hesitated, there was fire. Her breath came in pants now, and her dragon scratched at her skin, writhing to touch their mate. Pleading to ride him, to bite him. To claim him. Dragon or no, Kane was theirs.

How did she know? Because something deep within him was calling to her. It had been since the moment she'd locked eyes with him at the airport.

Kane's nostrils flared delicately, as if he was scenting her, and she could smell it, too. Her desire was clouding the air now.

His eyes blazed, and his devilish smile deepened. She was gone with that look. He could have whatever he wanted. He could have all of her—heart, body, thoughts, everything.

His lips crashed onto hers so hard she tasted blood, but it didn't deter her. No, it revved her up faster. Kane backed her against his Bronco and thrust his tongue past the closed seam of her lips. His grip was tight in the back of her hair, his body fluid against hers as he rolled his hips and hit her between the legs just right. She gasped when his lips brushed her neck just below her ear. He wrapped his arm around her back and pulled her closer as he rocked against her again. When his teeth grazed her neck at the next kiss, chills covered her skin.

She should be afraid of Kane, but she wasn't. Instead, her instincts were quiet, and her dragon was awed by him—watching, excited, ready.

Nothing had ever felt better in her life than Kane's biting kisses on her neck as he pulled the hem of her shirt up slowly, dragging his fingertips against her skin as he did. She wanted to bite him back so bad, but didn't trust herself. Dragon would take it too far, and Kane would balk. He would run, and just the idea of him disappearing from her life drew a long, low, prehistoric rumble from her chest.

Kane's hand went straight to her breast, cupped it hard, but she knew what he was doing. He was feeling the vibration of her growl there. A similar sound emanated from him, and she smiled up at the stars. Kane was wrong about his dragon being dead. He wasn't gone, just locked away by whatever those mad scientists had done to him. Dragon was calling to

The Darkness, urging him out of his cage, and that sound in his throat was proof there was life inside of Kane. Proof of life she should be terrified of, but that she was falling in love with instead. God, it was the sexiest sound she'd ever heard.

Bite him.

What?

Bite him. Bite, bite, bite. Bite him and make him ours.

Rowan shook her head hard, hoping to rattle Dragon off her quest.

Bite him!

With a snarl, Rowan turned in Kane's arms, pushed her ass against him seductively. He didn't hesitate, only pulled the bottom of her knit sweater until it was over her head and lying in the dirt near her feet. Her tank top came next, her bra un-snapped in the back, and then her black lingerie was in the pile with the rest. His lips were on the back of her neck again, working her skin to inferno. Teeth, teeth, suck. Rowan moaned. He owned her body right now. One hand massaged her breast while one traveled down her stomach, slipped into her jean shorts, and cupped her wet sex.

His erection was hard against her back. Kane pulled his lips from her neck just long enough to pull his shirt over his head with one hand, and now she could feel his fiery skin against her back. *Hello, Darkness.*

Rowan arched for him, slid her hands behind her and around his neck to keep him close. He growled again. *Darkness, Darkness. Dark Kane. Mine.*

Power pulsed from his skin, thickening the air, weighing heavy on her shoulders. She loved it. Loved that he was dominant. Loved that even though he couldn't call on his dragon, he could keep her safe. Safe, safe, safe. Such a beautiful, seductive word after feeling afraid for so long.

Kane ran his fingers down her wet folds, teased her entrance with a shallow touch. With his other hand, he grabbed her ass hard, squeezed and pushed her forward against the side of the Bronco. Oh he liked this—the control. He was going to take her from behind.

Rowan caught a glimpse of her reflection in the window. Hooded eyes blazing gold, lips parted, cheeks flushed. Kane's eyes glowed in the reflection as he gave her a slow, hungry smile that showed his white teeth. Monster. *Our monster.*

The sound of her button being undone made her close her eyes against the night, just to savor the seductive promise of that tiny *snap*. It had been so long since she'd felt adored like this. Eternity maybe. The slow *riiiip* of her zipper filled her head, and then the cool breeze was licking her skin as Kane shoved her shorts down to her ankles. She was wearing a black thong today, but Kane didn't just rip it off like she thought he would. Instead, he grazed his teeth over her hip as he bit the band. Hooking his fingers at the sides, he slowly pulled the panties down her curves, down her legs, his facial scruff scratching her skin the entire length.

A delicious shiver traveled from her ankles up her legs, up her spine, and landed in her shoulders. Her breath shuddered as she stepped out of the last stitch of her clothing. Kane's pants were next, but he gave his lips to the back of her neck as he moved, as he pushed his clothes down, unsheathing himself. God, how was he this smooth? This graceful? It was like his leg didn't hurt him at all right now. She hoped it didn't. She hoped she was the balm to his pain, as he was the cure to her fear.

His body warmth left her for a moment, and then Kane's jeans were in the pile with her discarded clothes. He told her so much with that. A smile stretched her lips, and she dared a look behind her. She wasn't just some fuck in an ally with his pants around his hips. She was something more—something special.

His eyes tightened in the corners, and he lifted his chin. Slowly, he dug his fingers into her hips and pulled her toward him, arched her lower back, gave himself access. And then he was there, poised at her entrance, in by an inch, teasing as his lips touched her again on the back of the neck. Teeth, teeth, teeth. *He wants to bite you, too.*

Rowan arched harder, instinctively, chasing him as he rocked gently away. Big, powerful man, his muscles rippling against her back as he rocked them both forward. He dragged his touch down her arm, intertwined their fingers and lifted her hand to the Bronco, braced her there. With his other, he took her hand and slid it down her stomach until she cupped herself. Until she could feel the swollen head of his cock right there, ready to plunge into her. Oh, he was going to make her feel this.

Teeth. He bit her shoulder almost hard enough to pierce her skin. With a gasp, she arched for him again.

"Do it," she begged. Do what? Bite her? Fuck her? Both felt right.

Kane plunged into her, stretching her with his width. He was almost too much. Almost too long, too thick, but she tried to relax. She could feel his graceful movement inside of her. Her fingertips brushed his shaft as he buried himself into her center.

Kane's breath came faster, and his body tensed against hers. "Fuuuck," he said in a shaky growl. And then he eased back and rammed into her again, harder. He pressed on her hand, made her touch herself as he went to work, filling her, depleting her, in and out until she was crying out with every stroke. Her legs didn't want to hold her anymore, but he kept her pinned against his Bronco, supporting her, holding her up as he bucked into her, his abs flexing against her back with the motion.

Something was happening. Something amazing that heated her middle like fire but didn't hurt. And there were his biting kisses again, but he wasn't teasing anymore. He clamped onto the back of her neck as he drove them to release. So vulnerable, having the Blackwing's teeth on the most sensitive part of her body, right on her spine. He could kill her with a bite, but he wouldn't. He wouldn't. Kane cared about her. He would take care of her and keep her safe.

But as he pumped into her harder and faster, as his body tensed and strained against her back, there was an instant she thought she'd made a dire mistake. With the first explosive pulse of her orgasm, Kane sank his teeth into her skin so deep, she gasped at the pleasure and pain. She thought he would end her. For a terrifying moment, she thought he would cut through her neck, but he didn't. Instead, he released her torn skin and yanked her against him, bucked into her, and gritted out her name. Warmth trickled down her neck, and it should've hurt. It should've ruined the moment, but instead, her release came even harder, blinding her with ecstasy. Kane swelled inside of her and shot warmth into her center. He was heavy, and so strong, and it was all she could do to keep herself braced against his car to give herself space to breathe.

"Kane, Kane," she said mindlessly as her orgasm

pounded through her.

He was emptying himself completely into her, and it was too much. It was trickling out of her, trickling down her legs to her knees. So fucking sexy. Kane grunted and bucked into her hard one last time.

And as Kane began licking the back of her neck, cleaning the blood, Rowan's body turned boneless. Her muscles twitched with the effort to remain standing. The bite mark stung, and his tongue against her torn skin burned, but she loved this. Loved his attention. Loved that he had claimed her just like a shifter. "You know what you just did, don't you?"

"I'm not sorry," he said in a gravelly voice she barely recognized.

Rowan gave a private smile. Maybe The Darkness was as enamored with her dragon as Dragon was with him. Dangerous, terrifying Blackwing Dragon had chosen his mate, and it was her. She stood there stunned as he cleaned her until the bleeding stopped and her accelerated healing sealed up the ripped skin. She hoped he'd done it deep so the scar would rise and be obvious.

She'd betrayed her people, betrayed her lineage, betrayed Damon, but in this moment, she couldn't gather the energy to care. She was happy. Not just happy, but for the first time in her life, she felt whole and brave. She felt ready for whatever came next.

As Kane pulled out of her, turned her slowly in his arms, and as he held her closer, she fell even harder. Why? Because that sexy rumble in his throat had softened to the hum that dragon shifters only let off when they were truly content. It matched hers.

Kane looked down at her, his dark eyebrows furrowed as if the sound unsettled him. As if he didn't understand it. But she did.

Their dragons were talking.

THIRTEEN

Kane stared at the red, angry wound he'd made on the back of Rowan's neck. He'd hurt her. What the hell had possessed him to do that? He hadn't been able to stop himself in the moment, and even now, he was having a damn hard time feeling anything but excitement.

Oh, he knew what claiming marks were. He just never in his life thought he would want to give one to a woman.

He dragged a washrag up her back where streams of warm water raced down her spine. He rested his arm on the edge of his bathtub, settled his chin on his forearm, and traced her smooth skin, drawing shapes as he connected water drops.

Rowan was sitting in deep water, resting her chin on her drawn up knees and staring off to the side with a dreamy look in her blue eyes.

"Are you angry?" he asked softly.

She inhaled suddenly. "Will you get in with me?"

Kane laughed, but Rowan cast him a serious glance over her shoulder. The amusement died in his throat. "My leg," he said through a frown.

"Take it off."

Kane swallowed his immediate instinct to deny her. He wanted to make Rowan happy, not take things away from her. With a sigh, he removed the prosthetic and eased into the steaming tub behind her. He was big and took up a lot of space, and the water rose to a couple inches below the rim. The warm water did feel good on his sore leg, and slowly, Rowan rested back against his chest, draped her hair over his shoulder languidly, and sighed out a contented sound. She seemed to need his touch as much as he needed hers.

God, this feeling in his chest. The hot one that eased when he was close to her like this. Kane rested his forehead against the back of her hair and nuzzled her gently. "That's not how I imagined it for our first time."

Rowan lifted her feet out of the tub and rested her crossed ankles on the rim, reached back and linked her fingers behind his neck, stretching out like a happy cat. "You picked me."

Kane kissed the claiming mark. "Yeah. I should've asked first though. I wasn't thinking."

"Do you regret it?"

"No." That was the easiest answer in the world. As of thirty minutes ago, he no longer felt alone in the world. It was a big deal. Consequences be damned, Rowan was his.

"Roe?"

"Hmmm?"

Kane cupped her full breasts gently and kissed her neck, then rested his chin on her shoulder. "Someday I'm gonna be good enough for you to claim me back."

"Kane," she said in a disapproving tone.

"No, just listen. I have a lot of work to do. You have this optimism I don't want to take from you. I'll work harder to spend time with the Bloodrunners for you. I'll hide less, okay? And someday when you think I'm ready, you can bite me back, and I'll be honored to have your mark."

"And what about when Harper has her baby and I go back to the Gray Backs?"

Kane's heart drummed with disappointment against his sternum. "When Damon finds out about you and I, he won't tolerate me in his territory. I can visit my mom and brothers, but taking up permanent residence? I can't pledge to the Gray Backs with you, Rowan."

"What do we do?"

"You stay, Roe. You stay here with me, with the Bloodrunners."

Rowan shook her head and hugged his hands to her chest. "When Harper gets her dragon back, I'll want to fight. It's too small a territory. My dragon will go to battle with hers. I can't be under another dominant dragon, Kane. I work best in the Gray Backs."

"What about your own mountains?"

"I'm listed as a problem shifter, remember? I can't get the land grants. Even if I could save up the money for a down payment, I can't get a loan. No one wants a problem shifter claiming land in their territory."

Kane closed his eyes and rested his lips right next to her ear. "What about my mountains?"

Rowan froze in his arms. "What do you mean?"

"This house is a mess, and I've been slowly working on fixing it up for three years. But I didn't buy this place for the house."

Rowan twisted in his arms, a frown marring her delicate blond eyebrows. "What are you saying?"

"I bought it for the land. I own this mountain and the next. Or I will when I pay the loan off. I can't get land grants either, so I bought what I could. It's nothing grand. It's not like Harper's territory, but maybe someday you could be happy here. With me."

Rowan parted her pretty lips in a shocked smile. "You love me," she accused, curling up her knees and turning all the way around to face him.

She damn near kicked him in the ball sack, so Kane cupped himself protectively. "Dammit, princess, watch the goods."

She tucked her knees to her chest and scooted closer. "You lo-ho-ho-ho-ooove me."

"I didn't say that." His cheeks were burning so he hid his gaze and his smile from her ridiculous accusations. "I love nothing."

"You just offered me your mountains. *Amore.* Oh, my God!" Her baby blues went round. "We have one of those epic love stories. I have to call Willa. We should get someone to write about us. Or like, make a poem. Bards can sing about us in castles for eternity. The Blackwing line finally fuses with the Bloodrunner line, ending a millennia-long war with love. Romeo and Juliet, but without the death part. With extra sex and more tattoos."

Kane laughed and splashed her. "I was being serious, you know. Now I take it all back. You can't share my mountains anymore."

"You wanna have my baaaaabies," she sang.

"Stop it," he said, blocking her tickling fingers while trying to keep his dick covered and protected from her kicking feet.

"You don't feel empty," she whispered suddenly, her eyes so round.

"What?"

"I was scared you would feel empty like with the other girls, but you gave me bites and mountains! Kane, do you know what this means?"

"That I enjoy sex with you?"

"Exactly, that we are meant to be!"

She was barely in control of her giggles and just being ridiculous now, so Kane splashed her.

Looking like a drowned rat, Rowen gasped. "Kane Metamucil Thunderdong."

"That's not even close to my name."

Rowan went crazy splashing, and for a moment, he just turned his head away and waited for her to tire herself out, but her giggles were infectious. So with a growl, he turned and went to town splashing her until they were both drenched and breathless from laughing. There was water all over the bathroom floor, and he was gonna have a hell of a time cleaning everything, but the beautiful smile on Rowan's face made everything worth it.

She moved onto his lap, straddling him, and pressed her breasts against his chest. Kane bit his bottom lip and slid his arms around her, pulled her right over his dick. It was hardening by the second. God, she was sexy. Playful and beautiful, her hair all plastered to her shoulders, make-up smudged, making the blue in her eyes look like ocean water. Her freckles on her nose were stark against her fair skin, and giggles were still bubbling up her throat. Fucking in a bathtub wasn't like the movies. It was raw. It was smeared make-up, confined space, and a sense of humor. It was working with the water waves to get off. It was fucking amazing. Rowan slid over him, and he rolled his eyes closed at how good she felt—how tight she was around his dick.

Kane gripped her hair and tasted her neck. Fuck, she smelled so good. Her neck was his favorite part about her. And yeah, he knew that messed with his man-card. He did love her tits and ass, but if he paid attention to her neck first, she got really wet and made these gaspy, little noises as if he could make her come with kisses. She was noisy with her pleasure, and so was her dragon. Rowan was close now. He could tell because she made this deep humming sound that he found so damn sexy he was gonna blow his load early if he wasn't careful.

He wanted a hard fuck. He wanted her fast, but Rowan was apparently in the mood for torture. She rocked her hips slowly, teasing him, barely lifting off his dick with each stroke, keeping him deep in her middle. He dug his fingers into her back and rammed her down harder on his lap, and she moaned like the little vixen she was. She drove him mad. All of his beating off to the thought of her didn't touch the real thing. His imagination sucked compared to how it really felt buried inside of her. Fuck, he needed more. Needed her bent over under him, or on all fours on the bathroom floor. He needed her on her back, driving into her, pounding her. Rowan clawed his back as she made little helpless noises deep in her throat. She liked it tight and deep then.

Rowan's orgasm came out of nowhere, pulsing hard around him, gripping him, pushing his own release. His balls clenched, and he shot into her, over and over with each hard stroke, until there was nothing left in him.

Going twice in a row like that, two hard fucks, had drained him. He sat in the tub twitching against her, clinging to her, face buried between her breasts because it was fucking paradise here. Lost in Roe. That's what this was. He could get lost in her arms and forget the pain, forget the darkness, forget everything but the blinding light she bathed him in.

And for a moment, as that strange humming vibrated from his chest, matching the sound that came from hers, he thought he could touch her dragon. And that was fucking magic. That was the closest he could get to the way he used to be. Rowan was a bridge to the life he wanted. A life he didn't deserve, but one he wanted to work toward.

Yeah, he wanted to give her his mountains. And yeah, he fucking loved his bite mark on her neck. Damon would kill him when he found out what he'd done, but this right here—this feeling of flying again—made it all worth it.

"You can have all of me." It was as close to *I love you* as he could get. He'd never uttered that before, not to anyone, but he hoped she understood the meaning that lay between his words.

And then she was crying. He wasn't sure at first, but she buried her face against his neck and went all soft, arms tucked between them, shoulders shaking, warm tears streaking down his arm. He didn't remember the last time he'd cried, so he worried he'd hurt her.

Cupping her neck, he eased her back so he could see her face. Her nose was red to match her cheeks, and her eyes were full of some deep well of emotion he couldn't identify. "Are you okay?"

"Yeah," she said thickly.

"What's wrong?"

She smiled, but her lips trembled, and tears ran

down her rosy cheeks.

Soft Roe, with the heart of a lamb.

Sweet Roe, who chose her people and held on.

Fierce Roe, who braved the lair of the Blackwing Dragon and didn't even smell scared at the deep rumbling in his chest.

Tender Roe, who shattered his glass heart when she whispered, "It's just that I love you, too."

FOURTEEN

Rowan rinsed the minty froth from her mouth and set the toothbrush Kane had given her beside his in the cup by the sink. He'd had one extra toothbrush. Color: black. Surprise, surprise.

"What's your favorite color?" she asked, snuggling back under the covers to watch him put on his prosthetic leg.

"Black like my soul," he quipped.

Rowan snorted. "I knew it. Are you sure you can't call in?"

"Princess, don't tempt me." Kane settled his jeans over the metal limb, and fastened them into place, then rolled over on the bed. With a grin, he bit her toe through the covers. "Martin needs the help."

"Your boss?"

"Yeah, he's up near retirement age, and he only has me and Wyatt working for him."

"You're a good person. You know how I can tell?"

Kane rolled his eyes and buried his face on the comforter beside her leg. "How," he asked in a muffled voice.

"Because you could get an all-day naked party with me, but you still won't ignore your responsibilities to Martin. I like that."

"He's been good to me," Kane said, resting his chin on her ankle. "He gave me a job knowing, or thinking, I was a dragon. Some people won't do that, you know? Some companies don't want to hire Supes. Martin hired two. Me and Wyatt."

"Are you and Wyatt friends?"

Kane lifted one shoulder up to his ear. "I guess he's the closest thing I have to one. Besides you. Do you need a ride home?"

"Will it make you late for work?"

Kane gave her a lopsided smile and nodded.

"Then no, I'll make like a dragon and fly. Harper said I need to make appearances in the sky every couple of days to remind people the Bloodrunners are protected. Two birds, one stone and all."

Kane pushed upward, his biceps bulging as he did. He stood to his full, imposing height and straightened his T-shirt—it was also black like his soul, as he liked to say. She giggled at the thought. Kane had a beautiful soul. He just liked to pretend he didn't.

"I left breakfast on a plate in the kitchen."

"You're trying to secure a blowjob, aren't you?"

Was that a blush on his cheeks? Kane grinned at the ground. "Uuuh. Sooo…" He ran his hand through his hair. He did that a lot when he was nervous or frustrated. He was being so damn cute right now Rowan had to pull the covers up to hide her smile.

"Maybe, do you want to go…eat food. Together? Like one of those…"

"Like a date?" Rowan scrambled up on the bed. She was wearing nothing but one of his T-shirts that hit at mid-thigh. "Are you asking me out on a date, Kane?" she asked too loud.

He hunched his shoulders like the pitch of her voice had hurt his ears. "I think I am."

Rowan let off a squeal and leapt at him.

"Oh, shit!" he said, catching her and losing his

balance. He reached back and steadied himself on the dresser and laughed against her neck. "Woman, give me warning. I have a bum leg, remember."

"My sexy-ass pirate." She kissed his lips and then nipped his bottom one as she pulled away. "Yes, yes, yes, I want to go eat food with you. Official date style. I'll wear something cute. I'll shave my legs! Can we take a picture together? This is a big deal, and a hundred years from now, I want to have a picture of the moment you asked me on our first date."

"A hundred years? Woman, when did we become immortal?"

Rowan scampered off and returned, held the phone up, kissed Kane on his cheek, and hoped he wasn't grimacing for the picture she took.

"Okay, I have to go." Kane kissed her gently, a soft chuckle in his throat. God, she adored that sound.

He still felt dominant and scary, but she was getting used to it little by little. Her dragon was adjusting, and it made it easier when he gave her easy laughs and smiles. She hugged his neck suddenly, snuggled close, and closed her eyes at how good it felt when he rubbed his hand up her back and hugged her tightly, as if he didn't want to let her go either.

"Does tonight work? I wouldn't mind seeing you again after I get off work."

"Will you pick me up like a real date and everything?"

"Yeah. I'll even say hi to the Bloodrunners when I come get you."

Rowan giggled and smiled so brightly at the wall behind him her cheeks hurt. He was going to try—for her.

"Um, Roe?"

"Yeah?"

"Can you not post that picture of us online? I need to make a few calls before we tell people. I need to make sure you are protected."

Rowan frowned. Protected? "Will people come after me?"

Kane shook his head, rasping his whiskers against her cheek. "I get attention, not the good kind, and I just want to make sure that doesn't blow over to you."

"Okay."

Kane eased back and lowered down, looked at her at eye-level. "It's not because I'm not proud as hell to have you with me. I swear it's not." His charming-boy smile curved his lips. "I'm gonna call my mom on the way to work and tell her about you. She's been afraid I would never find someone I cared about. She'll be happy."

Well, that did make her feel better. "So it's okay if I tell my people?"

The smile dipped from his lips, and his eyes went serious. "Give me a day before you start making phone calls. That's all I'm asking."

She pulled his palm to her lips and kissed it. "Okay, Blackwing, you have twenty-four hours starting now."

Kane winked at her—winked like a sexy-man!—and as Rowan stood there dumbfounded by his masculine beauty, he kissed her again, just a quick, affectionate peck, squeezed her ass hard, nipped her neck with a little growl, and limped out of the bedroom. Stunned, she followed him to the porch and waved him off as he sped out of the yard. He smiled in the rearview mirror at her and gave a two fingered wave out his open window just before he disappeared around a curve in the road.

It was in this moment, as she stood alone on his land for the first time, that it really struck her what had happened. Rowan stumbled onto the neatly mowed yard and rubbed the sore bite-mark on the back of her neck. She spun in a slow circle, stunned gaze on the surrounding forest and mountains. There was a chopping block and organized stacks of wood against one side of the house. An old tire swing hung from a towering white pine on the edge of the woods. From here she could see a babbling river running behind the house, and there was a hammock hung between two trees, creaking gently in the breeze. Birds chattered happily around her. Everything was lush, green, and beautiful. The run-down exterior of the cabin was what surprised her most about Kane's territory. She knew what it looked like inside. Rowan had expected it to look dilapidated inside to match the outside, but it wasn't. He was rebuilding it from the bones out. Last night, if she'd had her mind after being fucked so thoroughly by Kane in the front yard, she would've taken more time to appreciate the work he'd done.

Rowan padded over the sagging porch and pushed open the front door. The living room was stripped bare, down to the subflooring. The walls were open and exposed wiring hung from the rafters above. The couches were covered in plastic, and a TV was sitting on the couch cushions. But beyond that was a kitchen that had been remodeled from top to bottom. And she would bet her wings Kane had done all the work himself. It was small, but the wooden countertops were polished and the custom cabinets homey. It looked like a farm house kitchen with a big sink and everything. The bedroom and bathroom were also finished, down to the wood floors and polished log walls. The furniture was sparse, but tidy and well-placed, and made the rooms look bigger than they really were. The ceiling was sagging throughout the house, but already, Kane had written measurements and made notches all over the rotted rafters, and there was a ladder near the door with a measuring tape sitting on it.

What did it say about Kane that he only tackled one room at a time? It was apparent that he refused to move onto a new project until he was done with the last. Was it because that was how he handled his life? One day at a time? One obstacle at a time?

There was even a second bathroom off the only hallway. Rowan turned the knob and pushed open the door. Wait, this wasn't a bathroom at all. She stepped into a dark room and flipped on the light switch on the wall. A single light illuminated an office space. This wasn't like the rest of the house, though.

The floor was covered in dark carpet, and there were no windows. The ceiling was lower in here, as though this room had been some sort of add-on to the cabin. There was a massive three-monitor computer on a sprawling desk against the back wall. The desk was covered in stacks of notes. On the wall was nailed three cork boards with scribbled pieces of paper stuck with black push-pins. A map took up a good portion of the wall to her right, dotted in red sewing pins with thread connecting several of them to create a spider web effect.

This room wasn't homey. It was cold, like Damon and Clara's bedroom.

This wasn't an office. This was Kane's lair.

There was a glass display case of awards and medals he'd received from his time serving, but it was covered in a layer of dust. Perhaps he had hard feelings about all of it because of his leg. Or perhaps he was angry about having to fight after his dragon had been cut from him. There were a few pictures in the display. Kane in his combat uniform, holding an assault rifle, sunglasses hiding his eyes. One of him with a few other men, sitting in bag chairs in the sand, playing cards, dressed in desert fatigues, dog tags hanging from their necks. They were all smiling—all but Kane, who looked dead-eyed into the camera. And all their eyes were glowing inhumanly. Rowan gasped and wiped her hand across the thin layer of dust to see it better. Kane hadn't told her his team had been a task force of shifters. But really, Kane hadn't told her anything about this part of his life.

The edge of a picture on the first bulletin board fluttered in the breeze from the vent, demanding her attention. It was a picture of Kane kneeling down beside a wolf hound. The dog was giant and had his tongue flopped out the side of his mouth in a happy expression. Kane had his sunglasses on and was almost, *almost* smiling. The words *Gray Dog* were scribbled across the top in permanent marker. There was a yellow sheet of ruled paper underneath the picture with notes on it.

> *Killed June 11 by the Valdoro Pack*
> *Drake – Deceased, ashes, Harper*

Sam - Deceased, ashes, Harper
Ray - Deceased, ashes, Harper
Bryant - Deceased, ashes, Harper
Seth - dominant
Dustin - submissive
Jace – Second in the pack, dominant
Axton – Alpha, challenged outside of Drat's twice, bested him both, injured by Harper's fire, last seen outside of Tuscaloosa

Kane was hunting the pack. And rightly so. They'd killed his dog, and now the video cameras outside made sense. His explanation that he had to fight suddenly clicked into place. She hadn't taken it seriously enough. She'd thought it was just drunk asshole humans wanting to say they'd fought a dragon, but there were shifters challenging him, too. And Kane was fighting without an animal to call on. No wonder he'd stood his ground and gone on the attack as soon as he was tripped in the diner that first night. No wonder he dared Weston to come at him in the River's Edge last night. Showing fear would get him hurt or worse, so he'd trained himself to accept the brawl. To accept the chaos and pain because facing the challenger meant he had a chance at survival. Because shifters were different. If they sensed weakness, instinct took over. It was like this bloodlust, impossible to ignore. And even without his dragon, Kane was still here, still mostly whole, still holding his own.

She skimmed lists of names and places. Kane had constructed archives of all known crews within a hundred-mile radius and had write-ups on every member. He had pictures that looked like he'd pulled them off surveillance cameras at gas stations and street corners, and some of the logos on the pictures looked official.

Slowly, Rowan sat in the computer chair. She systematically read through the piles of notes. Time dragged on and on until the notes stopped making sense. The words became too big, and some were just sheets of numbers. She was stuck—a sponge left thirsty for more knowledge.

On the far edge of the desk was a large monitor with the views from two outside cameras, focused on his front yard and front porch. There were three others he'd put in the woods somewhere. One was a clear view of the entrance to his property, angled right at the full mailbox. The edge of one of the junk-mail magazines was hanging out and fluttering in the breeze. Rowan frowned at the blank computer monitor. When she bumped the mouse, a blue screen asking for a password came up.

She should stop here, but curiosity had sunk it's long, sharp claws into her. She'd learned more about Kane in the last few minutes than she had since she'd met him.

One password, and if it wasn't meant to be, she would take it as a sign.

Rowan leaned forward, fingers poised over the keyboard. It would be something he kept to himself. Something he wouldn't have shared with anyone.

Fingers shaking, she typed *thedarkness*. Enter.

The blue morphed to a screen covered in open tabs, and she huffed a surprised sound. She couldn't believe it had worked.

The front window had a picture of Kane, but he looked different. He was a teenager in it, his dark hair cropped close to his scalp. And his eyes…they were a soft brown. They looked human. This must've been taken before the genetic cleansing, when he and The Darkness still worked together and shared his body.

Rowan squinted and read the official report. *Apex Genetic Testing* was typed into the logo along the top.

Kane Reeves
Age: 18
Height: 6'2"
Shifter Status: Intact, Dragon, Lethal
Cleansing by court order, one year maximum, put-down order in place

"Jesus," she whispered. She minimized the screen and read the next. It was a list of medications. The next was a schedule of experiments he went through over a four-month slot of time. There were notes in bubbly letters from a nurse named Wendy Sanger.

Not working. Dragon is fighting. Hardest case so far.
Kane attacked the therapist today. Changed and nearly killed him. Placed in seclusion for one week.

The next window was the list of experiments he endured for the next four months. They looked more intensive, and there was a follow-up picture. Kane looked skinnier, his cheeks hollow, and his eyes...one was frozen green, one was soft brown. He stared at the camera with a look like he wanted to die.

Bile crept up the back of her throat, and the first tear streamed down her cheek. Her heart felt like it was ripping in two inside of her chest cavity.

Another list of experiments and meds for the last four months. Wendy's notes had gotten desperate.

In seclusion full-time. Out of control. Changes constantly. He's getting too big for the facility. Too strong for the chains. His shifter healing is slowing, but the put-down order is coming up too quick. He's a good kid, I can see it. The dragon is fighting so hard. Killing him. This one will hurt. We lost Brandon last week, and now Kane? I'm doing everything I can but if his dragon doesn't give up, he will be gassed two weeks from tomorrow. I've put in my resignation. I can't do this anymore.

That was the last entry from Wendy. The next window was a picture of Kane with his hair shaved and a trio of deep scars down the side of his head. His eyes were dead and blazing green, and he was leaning back on the wall, chin lifted, staring at the camera like he hated everything. He looked exhausted and emaciated. He looked like he had nothing left to lose. Nothing to live for.

The next note was in new handwriting—block letters, all neat and perfectly kerned. *Apex has cleansed its first dragon. Success. Kane will have a shot at a normal life now, and Apex was given a sizable grant by the government to continue the program. The team and I feel good about the work we've done here.*

Rowan clicked out of that one as fast as she could because the words ripped her guts out. They'd done good? He could lead a normal life? They'd tortured him until his dragon was made so small, and so weak, that Kane couldn't find him anymore.

The next screen was a typed list of names.

Holly Dunes – lion, killed in transition
Brandon Fastmen – wolf, killed in transition
Meghan Stewart – grizzly bear, killed in transition
Dawn Evener – grizzly bear, no trace of animal, married, two human children
Kannon Dayton – wolf, deceased, took life

Kiera Pierce – lion, no trace of animal, never married, never registered to a pride, no children

Caleb Porter – panther, killed in transition

Ben Porter – panther, last seen in Bilk Creek Mountains. On the move. In hiding. Married. Mated? Animal? One child. Human? Shifter? No established contact.

Where the fuck are you, Ben?

LSKDJFLSKJFDLKF

The last line looked like it was typed in anger. In utter frustration. Kane was looking for Ben Porter, but why?

"It wasn't all bad," Kane murmured from behind her.

Rowan startled so hard, she nearly fell out of the chair. "Kane! Oh, my gosh, I'm so sorry." She patted the stacks of notes around her, trying to organize them.

"It's fine." Kane's eyes were dead, though, like his picture at Apex Genetic Testing. He stood leaning against the door with a bag of take-away food in his hand, arms crossed over his chest like a shield. "You guessed my password."

"Kane, I'm really sorry. Please forgive me. I didn't come in here to invade your privacy." She approached him slowly, held her hands out, palms open. "I-I thought it was a bathroom, and I wanted to see the work you'd done on the house, but it was your office. I started looking at your pictures, and it felt like a connection to you. Like the pieces you hide from me, but it's not right what I did. I took pieces of you before you were ready to share. Please, Kane. Please forgive me."

He cleared his throat and wouldn't meet her eyes, and now her heart hurt even worse somehow.

"I came back hoping you would still be here. Have you been in my office this whole time?"

"This whole time? What time is it?"

"I left four hours ago."

"Shit. I completely lost track of time."

Kane huffed an angry breath and chewed on his bottom lip, gaze still on the wall. The air felt so heavy and thick it was hard to breathe. When a warning growl rumbled from him, Kane shook his head hard, cut off the noise. With a deep frown, he said, "I think you should go."

"Kane, please," she begged, tears streaming

down her cheeks. "I love you more now. Everything I learned about you, I love you more." She clutched his shirt in desperation. "I won't ever come in here again if you don't want me to. Please don't push me away."

Bite him. Bite him now before he runs.

"Stop it."

Kane jerked his glowing green eyes to her. "What?"

Rowan pushed up on her tiptoes and kissed him hard. She pushed her tongue past his closed lips in desperation. Moments drifted by, and Kane stood there like an immoveable stone. Eventually though, he softened, moved his lips against hers and drew her against his body, harder and harder until her bones ground. The bag of food hit the floor. The growl in his throat grew louder and more terrifying. The air became nearly unbreathable. Kane pushed her until her back hit the wall hard. He didn't bother taking off her sleep shirt, and she wasn't wearing panties. Kane simply pulled her knees around him, jerked the button of his jeans open and thrust into her roughly, held there for a second, then bit her bottom lip hard enough to draw blood and slammed into her again.

He was worked up, angry with her, and she'd

known provoking him would get her a hard fuck, but that's what she wanted right now. She would take anything, as long as he wasn't giving up on her.

He held the backs of her knees, and his arms bulged and flexed as he slammed into her faster. She was already close. She shouldn't have been. This should've been an anger-fuck just for Kane, but he was hitting her just right, and that sound in his throat was so sexy, so consuming, that she was already on a high from the oncoming release.

"Harder," she screamed, and with a snarl, he reared back and bucked into her again and again and again until she was arching her spine against the wall in desperation.

When her orgasm shattered her body, she dug her nails into his back as hard as she could. Heat blasted through her chest. It was excruciating. It was beautiful. It was everything.

Kane gritted his teeth and grunted, froze buried deep inside of her. Warm seed shot into her, filled her, and he bucked erratically until the throbbing sensation stopped.

She thought he would drop her to the floor and walk out like she deserved, but he didn't. Chest heaving, he pressed himself against her, hugged her, buried his face against her neck and whispered, "I'm sorry."

And now Rowan wanted to cry again because this wasn't the outcome she'd wanted. She didn't want him to feel guilt. She rolled her head back until it hit the wall, and she ran her fingers through his mussed hair. "You have nothing to be sorry for. I'm the one who messed up."

Kane pulled her off the wall and hugged her tightly against him until his breathing evened out. "You wouldn't have been so curious if I would've told you any of this. I'm just not used to..."

"Sharing?"

He chuckled a single, exhausted sound. "Yeah. Communication isn't my strong suit, princess. I want to tell you things. I want to share my past, but it's gonna be slow-going with me. You're gonna have to be patient."

"Who is Ben Porter?"

Kane sighed and lowered her to the ground, then fastened his pants. "Ben was my friend in Apex. The cleansing process was horrible, and painful. It was torture, but the nurses tried to make the in-between okay for us. On days I had control of the dragon, I got to eat my meals in this cafeteria with the other kids. We became friends. No one else in the whole world was ever going to be able to understand what we went through in that facility. Some of the kids were sad and homesick. Hurting. They usually didn't make it. Ben was funny, and even when he felt like shit, he told jokes. Mostly dirty ones. Ryder reminds me of him. Because his animal fought like mine did, he had to stay for eight months, so we got to know each other well. He told me one night while we were all getting ready for bed that the cleansing wasn't permanent. Not for him. He said some man called him in the middle of the night the month before his adoptive parents put Ben and his brother in the program. He said the man told him he'd had a dream about him, about his panther, and he said not to worry because his life would get good again. That he would find his animal again. And then he hung up. Ben was convinced he just had to get through the pain and that, someday, when he wasn't a minor anymore, he would figure out how to get his panther back, and no one would be able to take him away again. Except Ben's brother, Caleb, died in there. The cleansing did that sometimes. Took the animal but took the human, too, you know? Ben stopped joking, stopped fighting, and his animal went really quick after that. He was taken away. No goodbye, nothing. I was just alone with the new kids who were all afraid of me. The staff at Apex put me in solitary soon after. I thought the man on the phone with the prediction was just Ben's way of dealing with what we were going through, but then last year, Wyatt got drunk one night and told me about these predictions Beaston had made about him."

Chills rippled across her skin when he said Beaston's name. He was a Gray Back, like her, and she'd grown up with him in her crew. Beaston could see things across the veil. He could see future things like Weston, his son, could.

"I started thinking maybe he was the one who called Ben. I started hoping that maybe Ben had found his animal again. That he was okay somewhere."

"If it was Beaston who called him," Rowan whispered, "then Ben *will* find his panther again. Beaston's never wrong. Kane?"

"Yeah?"

"Do you want your dragon back?"

He backed away from her by a step. "I don't know."

"Why not?"

"Because my dragon wasn't a good animal to have, Rowan. He was a monster. Checking on Ben isn't about me. It's not so I can be a shifter again. It's so I can make sure my friend is alive and okay. At least one of us made it, you know? Found a good life."

"But you said you missed him. That you missed flying and breathing fire."

"Yeah, and what's good for me isn't necessarily good for the rest of the world."

"You're stronger now, Kane. You could control him."

"Fuck, Rowan, stop! It's not even an option, and Ben was probably just talking out of his ass."

"Ignoring everything else, if you could have him, would you want your dragon back, Kane?"

He stared at the computer screen, at the picture of him with the empty eyes and the scars on his shaved head. His lips thinned into a grim line, and he refused to answer.

"Kane," she murmured, gripping his shirt. "If you

could control the dragon, and the world was safe from him, would you want him back?"

Kane pulled away from her, picked the bag of takeaway food off the ground, then disappeared down the hallway.

And that was answer enough. That was a yes. If it was a hard no, he would've just said it. But he hadn't answered because she would've heard the lie in his voice.

Rowan frowned at the computer, at the broken face of her mate in the days after he'd lost his animal. He still got that expression sometimes when she talked about her dragon with him. That broken, yearning look in his eyes, and she couldn't live her whole life stomaching that kind of pain in the man she loved.

She had to find Ben Porter.

FIFTEEN

Kane slipped out from under the covers of 1010, the cabin Rowan had moved into in Harper's Mountains. He'd taken Rowan out to eat in Bryson City, and she'd begged him to stay. But when he'd fallen asleep beside her, curled around her soft body, he'd dreamt of flying. He'd dreamt of fire. He'd dreamt of the mountains glowing red and billowing smoke and then had woken up in a cold sweat.

It was Rowan's magic, or perhaps being in Harper's Mountains, that was dredging up the awful vision. Or perhaps it was 1010. Weston had told him to "sleep well" with his lips all twisted up like he knew something Kane didn't.

Fuckin' Novak Raven and his riddles lately. He'd

been standoffish from the time Kane had brought Rowan home and then throughout the bonfire the Bloodrunners had built before Kane led an exhausted Rowan inside 1010. Over the fire, Weston had watched him with his eyes darkened to raven black, his head cocked like a bird, the set of his mouth grim. It put some deep-growing instinct inside of Kane on edge.

Novak could kill him. Any of these shifters could if they knew how weak he was. Surrounding himself with Bloodrunners had always put his hackles up. Sure, they were nice enough people, but they were a breed governed by their animals, and this crew had some of the most dominant bloodlines in the entire world. And what had his dumb ass done? Claimed their protector.

He strapped his prosthetic on as quietly has he could, then clad in only his briefs, strode out into the living room. There had been a delivery today from the airline, but Rowan had put off showing him her treasure.

She should've learned her lesson from earlier, though. Hiding only made both of them more curious, and now he couldn't stop himself. It was almost like he was possessed, and his body moved of its own accord.

Beckoning him, the large, purple suitcase sat against the back wall of the house. *Open me. See what your mate attached to. See what she would sicken for. See what she would die for.*

Kane narrowed his eyes at the luggage and let off a low rumble. He hated whatever was in that case. Hated it because she had chosen it before she'd ever met him.

She didn't wait for us.

Fuck, what was wrong with him?

His stride was in jerks, and when he stepped wrong on his bad leg, he had to right himself on the back of the couch.

The suitcase was pulsing. *Come closer.*

Kane gritted his teeth and clenched his hands, but didn't stop until he was standing over the luggage. Slowly, he knelt down and crushed the lock in his hand, threw it onto the floor, and unzipped the case slowly.

He inhaled deeply before he lifted the lid and shoved it back.

A large piece of metal lay inside, folded in half

and melted on one side.

Kane ran his hand over his face, trying to figure out why Rowan would attach to a piece of junk instead of the treasures of old. He'd expected bricks of gold or precious gems. Something of value, not a twisted, melted hunk of metal. And then it hit him. The story of Rowan's kidnapping. Of how she'd almost died by Damon's dragon fire. Of how her father, Creed, had covered her with metal that was too small to cover his massive grizzly body but that had kept Rowan safe.

Kane looked back over his shoulder at the open doorway of the dark bedroom. Rowan was breathing deeply, sleeping soundly, and he was sitting here hating a piece of metal for taking a piece of her heart.

God, he had to do better than this. Had to take better care of her. He needed to protect her treasure so she wouldn't get The Sickening again. He studied the gnarled metal. Three seconds. She'd said it was just a few seconds, and Damon's fire had nearly melted straight through the metal.

Something deep and dark inside of him unfurled. *That's not her treasure. We are.*

Kane clenched his fists hard to punish the tiny

voice that was fucking with his head. Maybe he was losing his mind. He was imagining The Darkness. Wishing for his return badly since he'd started hunting Ben. This wasn't his dragon, though. The voice was too small, too frail, with the power of a gnat. No, this was a figment of his imagination. This was being around Rowan's dominant dragon and wanting so desperately to be worthy of her.

Kane slammed the lid on the suitcase, stood, and strode for the front door. He grabbed his phone off the table where he'd left it by his keys and made his way outside. The night air had a bite to it and cooled his molten body a few degrees. He inhaled deeply and cleared his head.

He'd asked Rowan for a day because of this call. Because he needed time to man up and put himself on the radar of the blue dragon before he found out about Kane claiming his great granddaughter.

Damon Daye was going to kill him. All Kane could do was ask for more time with Rowan and hope the old dragon forgave his lineage and understood love.

Kane snorted and shook his head at the full moon that sat low over the Smoky Mountains. A minute ago, he'd been contemplating his hatred over Rowan's treasure, and now he was going to ask Damon to let him have her for a little while?

Irritated with himself, Kane connected a call on his cell to the one number in his phone he'd never dared to call. This was his 911. This was the number he'd kept all these years in case he lost control again and needed to make sure the world was safe from him.

Damon would've put him down.

"Hello?" a smooth, deep voice answered on the other line.

"Damon Daye?" Kane asked, narrowing his eyes at the moon.

There was a long hesitation and then, "Blackwing Dragon. I've waited a long time for this call."

Kane frowned and ran a hand down his chin in a nervous gesture he'd picked up from the time he'd spent in Apex. "You know me?"

"Yes. I've watched you."

"To make sure I didn't turn out like my father?"

Damon chuckled darkly. "No. I've watched you to make sure you were good enough."

Kane scratched the back of his head and sat on the edge of the porch. "Good enough for what?"

"For Rowan."

"I don't understand. Did Beaston tell you about us?"

"Feyadine told me about you. Do you know her story?"

Kane had done his research. "She was your first mate. She came between you and my father hundreds of years ago, back when you were still immortal."

Damon swallowed audibly through the line. "Very good. Feyadine was a seer. She could see things like Beaston can. Like Weston can. And one night while she was sleeping beside me, she had a dream."

"What kind of dream?"

"She dreamt of the Blackwing crest and the Bloodrunner crest side-by-side in a ring of fire. She told me that the two lines would fuse."

"Hundreds of years ago, she predicted this?" Kane's body was covered in gooseflesh now.

"I thought she'd been wrong about this vision. I thought Marcus was dead and that I was the last immortal dragon. And when he died his final death, I thought the same again. There would be no fusing of the ancient clans. And then there came you. A Blackwing not five years older than Rowan. One with a dragon to match hers."

"I don't have the dragon anymore."

"But you're still her match."

"I want to be. I do. But I can practically see her destiny and how strong she'll be, and I will hinder her. I'll hold her back. I'll be this crippled human she has to drag through life, always protecting."

"Does she feel like that? Does she see you as some crippled human?"

Kane picked up a stick off the porch and chucked it into the dark woods. "She sees what she wants to see. Can I ask you something?"

A low rumble sounded over the phone, and something terrible and dark drew up within Kane. He asked anyway. "Did you have anything to do with my dragon being taken?" It would've been perfect for Damon. The last of his enemies rendered helpless. The last Blackwing Dragon snuffed out, and Damon didn't even have to lift a claw to do it.

"Marcus was my friend for hundreds of years before he betrayed me for the first time, Kane."

"Just answer the question."

"You're breathing because of me, boy. Your dragon killed that black bear shifter. And yeah, he had it coming. He couldn't ruin a human's life like that and get away with it. He would've been dealt with, but you were too loud about it. You damn near burned the entire neighborhood that night. Do you remember anything?"

The blood was draining from Kane's face and hands, leaving his skin clammy. "No." His voice broke on the answer.

"I do. I was there to bring you back down to earth and force you to Change back because I could see it in your eyes. Your dragon was alone, in control, without you there to guide him. And he was scorching the land. Do you know what your sentence was supposed to be? Do you?" he barked into the phone. "Death, Kane. You were supposed to be shipped to a shifter prison and put down humanely, and your body was to be burned and your ashes dumped in the ocean. I fought hard for you because I could see it. Rowan had been kidnapped and was broken. She wasn't going to come out of my mountains, and you were on a collision course with the government. I trusted Feyadine, I trusted

Beaston, and they'd both had the same dream centuries apart, and her father, Creed, was begging me to save you. *Save that boy*. I went to battle to get you a year in Apex. It's not what I wanted. I wanted you to be able to keep your dragon and learn to control him, but no amount of money I could throw at the courts was going to save him. It was you or the dragon, Kane. Rowan was clinging to her fear so hard, a dragon stuck in the body of a mouse, and her shot at breaking out was you. And all the while you were being stripped of your dragon, I was praying to God every night that you were strong enough to survive it because someday, somehow, you were going to help my—" Damon's voice cracked, and he inhaled a deep, shaky breath before he tried again. "That you were going to help my broken girl. Have you bitten her yet?"

Kane was shocked. It was all too much. Too much to learn all at once. He was breathing because of Damon? He was breathing because of Rowan? So much pain to get here…

"You should've let me die," he whispered.

"Don't you fucking say that to me. You didn't break, Kane. Not even close. And someday you'll be looking in the eyes of your mate, holding your first child against your chest, and you're going to look back on this moment and regret that statement. Your journey to that moment, all the heartache and pain, will be worth it. Did. You. Bite her?"

"Yes," Kane answered on a breath.

"Good. She doesn't belong in my mountains anymore, Kane. She belongs in yours."

And then the line went dead.

SIXTEEN

"Tell me I'm doing the right thing," Rowan said.

"You're doing the right thing," Air Ryder said around a giant bite of submarine sandwich. A tomato slice squirted out the end and onto the floorboard of the rental car. "What are we doing again?" he asked, slurping lettuce strands like spaghetti noodles.

Rowan glared. "I didn't even know they made two-foot-long sandwiches."

"Yeah…well…if a sandwich is shorter than my dick, it ain't worth eating."

"God," she muttered with an eye roll. They were currently sitting in the car on the edge of the Red Havoc Crew territory.

The big cats tended to be ridiculously territorial,

and here she was a six-hour drive away from Harper's Mountains, headed to the heart of a notoriously reclusive crew. Why? Because between her, Bash of the Boarlanders, and Damon, they had tracked Ben Porter to a possible unregistered member of this crew who went by the name Benson Saber. She'd planned on coming alone, but Ryder had relentlessly annoyed her until she gave in and invited him.

He wasn't even being protective like Weston. Nope. He just wanted to get out of work at Big Flight ATV Tours for the day and eat copious amounts of road-food. He'd practically made a quilt out of empty beef jerky packages.

"So," Ryder said, licking his fingers loudly. "Are we gonna have to like…fight? Because I'm good with that."

"No! Ryder, don't start a fight. We need information, that's all. Pinky swear me." She jammed her pinky at him. "Do it."

The redheaded muscle man pouted but hooked his pinky around hers. They'd done that a hundred times growing up. Pinky swears were binding.

"Why aren't you wearing a shirt?"

Ryder swallowed a massive bite like a python and looked at her like the answer should be obvious. "For pictures."

Rowan didn't even want to know what he meant by that, so she got out and made her way toward the first small cabin in a row of ten. Ryder followed behind her, still eating the massive sandwich. At least he looked less threatening cradling a meal. His muscles were bulging out everywhere without his shirt to cover them, but he looked harmless enough when he talked to his tomato slices, encouraging them to "stay between the buns."

She lifted her hand to knock on the door, but just as her knuckles graced the wood, a scuffle sounded behind her and something cold and unforgiving shoved her head forward. The click of a gun was loud in the quiet of the surrounding woods.

"Drop it, or I'll pop your head off your body, fuckwad," Ryder gritted out.

Rowan lifted her hands in surrender and turned slowly to face the gun. Ryder stood there, triceps straining with the grip he had on the giant's neck who had the gun trained on Rowan. His sandwich was on the ground, and his eyes blazed the gold of his inner snowy owl.

"Please don't hurt us," Rowan said, her voice trembling. "I just came to talk to Benson Saber.

The man had a single scar down his face, right through his eye, and they were as gold as Ryder's with tiny pupils. Panther. His crop of dark hair was mussed, and he wore a sweater riddled with holes. He smelled of fur and dominance.

When he spoke, his voice came out a feral snarl. "Ain't no Benson here. Leave."

"Please," she whispered. "I'm desperate. If he's here, can you tell him I'm friends with Kane Reeves?"

"Barret, it's okay," a deep voice said.

Barret the Titan un-cocked his gun and dropped it to his side at the same time Ryder released his throat. Exposing his neck to the man that had approached from around the side of the cabin, Barret backed up a few steps.

Rowan had seen a group picture with Benson and his brother Caleb flanking Kane in a cafeteria, and she canted her head at how familiar this man looked. He was just like his picture. Same eyes, same blond hair, same build. "Ben?" she asked.

"Is Kane dead then?" Ben asked, crossing his

arms over his chest and splaying his legs like he expected bad news.

"No," she whispered. "He's been looking for you."

"And yet he's not the one standing in my territory. You are."

"Your territory? You're alpha here?"

He narrowed his blue eyes suspiciously. "Why are you smiling like that?"

"Because I'm happy you're okay. Kane...he has fond memories of you."

Ben snorted. "You're mistaken, lady. There are no fond memories from the hell I met the dragon in."

Other men were starting to gather now, crowding in closer. Three of them held handguns casually by their sides.

"Uuh, is there somewhere we can speak in private?" she asked.

Ben took his time answering. He cast Ryder a hard glance. "How do you two know Kane?"

"Fourth best friend," Ryder said without hesitation, raising his hand like a school kid.

Rowan internally groaned and turned slowly, lifted her long hair off her neck to show him the bite mark. When she turned back around, Ben wore a slight smile.

"Kane's mine," she murmured.

"They're all right," Ben said, power pulsing in his voice. He twitched his head toward the row of cabins. "Follow me."

Ben's crew crowded together, watching them leave, and it lifted the hairs on Rowan's neck to give them her back. Ryder bumped Barret hard in the shoulder as he passed and said, "You owe me four-ninety-five for that sandwich, Dick."

She couldn't tell for sure, but she thought Ben chuckled ahead of them. He pushed open the door of the largest cabin, third in line. He gestured for them to sit down at a table, and as she and Ryder settled in the uncomfortable wooden chairs, Ben poured something clear and pungent from a ceramic jug into a trio of small mason jars.

"Fuck yes," Ryder said, taking one of the glasses from Ben. "Can I make the toast?"

Looking amused, Ben cocked a blond eyebrow. "Go for it."

"To not having to break my pinky promise to this wee beasty," he said with a nod of his head at Rowan.

They drank up, and Rowan coughed over and

over at the sting of the moonshine. Someone had made this batch super-fucking-strong.

"Beasty?" Ben said. "You don't smell like a shifter."

"Yeah, dragon scales don't have a scent," Ryder said. "You probably already know that from being friends with Kane."

"A dragon then? A Bloodrunner?"

Rowan nodded once and smiled.

"Well holy fuckin' shit, he found you then."

"What do you mean?"

"I always thought it would take a special brand of tough to catch the Kane. I imagine he's not an easy man to love."

"Easy for me."

"Hmm," Ben said through a tight smile. "Why are you here, Bloodrunner?"

"I came to ask for myself if the prediction ever came true."

The smile fell from Ben's face so fast his ears moved with it. "Don't know what prediction you're talking about."

"I think you do. Was it Beaston? I asked him, but he went all tight-lipped."

Ben gave his attention to the wall. She'd seen this tactic before from Kane, but she could be patient.

"How is Kane?" he asked in a careful tone.

"He's okay."

Ben's eyes tightened at the lie in her voice. "There's a reason men like him and me are better off under the radar, you understand? Outing him could get him killed. Outing me will get *you* killed."

"Party foul," Ryder said. "No threats. Minus four points for the panther."

"I'm not a panther."

"Horseshit, you smell like fur, and you're alpha of a panther crew. If it walks like a duck and fucks like a duck..." Ryder tipped up the mason jar and gulped the leftover drops of moonshine.

"Is it science?" she asked. "Did you find the cure? Or...the un-cure?"

Ben huffed an angry laugh and leveled her with a fiery glare. His eyes looked lighter, but still within the realm of human. "Trust me when I say, you don't want to pull the tail of Kane's dragon. You haven't seen him before. I have. If it was any other shifter from Apex that had been stripped, I'd try to help, but Kane isn't like the rest of us. He's better off alone, and his dragon is better off dead."

"I can help him."

"You can't."

"I can! He's stronger now. He can control it."

Ben shook his head for a long time, and his eyes looked hollow, as if remembering Apex again. "You don't know what you're asking, Bloodrunner. You know when people talk about the end of days?"

"Yeah?"

"In Apex, that's what they called Kane's dragon. End of Days. Do the world a favor. Do Kane a favor and don't revive the damn apocalypse."

Rowan swallowed hard. "You're saying it's possible, though."

"Woman, are you hearing me?"

"I love him, Ben. He's not the same kid from the facility anymore. He survived the cleansing, he survived war, he survived countless fights, and infinite loneliness. He didn't find a crew like you to lean on. He's been out there by himself this entire time *owning* it. Kane is a badass, but you have to understand, he's still empty. He's missing his animal. Best case scenario, he lives a half-life until he draws his last breath, and I'll be there, every moment, watching the yearning in his eyes every time I shift without him. I'll have to watch him go pale every time our friends talk about their animals because it's a reminder that he's on the outside. You have yours back. You got lucky. Kane is still walking this world as a ghost. Do you remember what it felt like when you lost the panther? That bone-deep hollowness? He's still in that all these years later, and it's not getting better, Ben."

Ben twirled his empty mason jar around and around between his fingers, staring at it, his face green as if he was sick just thinking about the ache.

The door swung wide open, streaming sunlight, and a little boy of five or six barreled in and crashed against Ben. He caught him and hugged him tight, tried to shield the little boy from Rowan, but she'd already seen his eyes. Bright gold. Little brawny panther cub, and he was towheaded just like his father.

A woman stood in the doorway, a questioning look on her face. "Hello," she said softly.

"Jenny, take him in the back room," Ben said.

With a frown, Jenny held out her hand to the little boy. "Come on, Raif. Let's go change out of your swimsuit."

The skinny little kid waved shyly as he passed Rowan, and when she looked back at Ben, there was no denying the animal inside of him. His eyes were bright like the sun. Like Ryder's were right now. Like his son's.

"I trust you not to tell a soul, or the government will have a team down in my territory within the day. I'm alive because I'm a secret, you understand? The cleansing didn't take with me, and they'll have me back in Apex, experimenting, seeing where they went wrong. I have a good life here. I'm happy."

"I swear I won't tell a soul other than Kane. You have my word as a Bloodrunner. I'll keep your secret safe, Ben. You were kind to Kane in Apex. You made his time there bearable. It's the least I can do."

"And you?" Ben said gruffly to Ryder.

Ryder held out his pinky. "I pinky swear not to tell anyone."

Ben frowned, unimpressed, but he locked pinkies anyway. "I think you should both go now."

"Yeah," Rowan said, her disappointment infinite. She had gotten some answers, but not the important one.

Ben followed them out and stood in his open doorway as they walked away. "Tell Kane I said thanks."

"For what?" Rowan asked softly.

"For being there for me when Caleb died."

With a sad smile, she murmured, "Sure. I'll tell him."

"Bloodrunner?"

"Yeah?" she asked, turning around again.

She wiped her burning eyes and hated how weak she felt. Ben just stood there as moments dragged on, his head tilted, eyes watching her. At last he said, "It's not science." He pulled his shirt to the side and exposed deep scars that looked like they were made from fangs. A claiming mark. "It's love that'll bring on the End of Days."

SEVENTEEN

The *chop, chop* of wood echoed down the winding dirt road to 1010. Rowan was sitting on the front porch lacing up her hiking boots, but at the sound, she scanned the woods up by Weston and Ryder's cabins. The Novak Raven was cutting wood, probably for another bonfire tonight since it wasn't cold enough for flames in the hearths yet.

Or maybe it was. She ran hot, and autumn was fast approaching the Smoky Mountains.

Flip-flap. Rowan frowned up into the tree branches across the dirt road, and there was Avery, landing on a low-hanging tree branch. Rowan's relationship had grown with the Bloodrunners, and she'd found her tentative place. She'd grown to love the mates her friends had chosen, but for some reason, Avery and Weston had kept her at arm's length. It was something she thought about way too damn much because she was a people pleaser. She didn't like the thought of someone disliking her, and it had never been like this between her and Weston before.

They'd grown up in the same crew. From birth, they'd been friends. More like siblings, so his hesitation around her hurt.

Avery hopped down to an even lower branch and cocked her head, her black feathers shining like silk in the evening sunlight.

Rowan pushed off the porch and jogged down the stairs. And with only a slight hesitation, she risked rejection and held her forearm out, stood still as a stone.

Avery canted her head the other way, then spread her massive wings and soared toward Rowan. For a moment, she thought Avery would attack and pull up at the last moment, but she didn't. She landed on her arm, claws digging into her skin enough to draw blood. Avery was big, almost as big as Weston's raven, but she was still light enough for Rowan to carry comfortably.

"I'm supposed to be the one to fix things between me and Wes, aren't I?" she asked, stroking a knuckle down Avery's smooth, feathered back.

"Caw!" Avery left her beak open, panting, her dark eye locked on Rowan.

"Right." Balancing the raven on her arm, Rowan strode up the road.

Weston wasn't wearing a shirt. None of the boys did around here, but then again, they never had. Clothing hindered shifts, so they wore less. His arms and chest were covered with tattoos, and his suntanned skin glistened with sweat as he drew the ax back and slammed it into a log on the chopping block.

He looked up long enough to cast a greeting smile to his mate on Rowan's arm, but he didn't spare the same courtesy to her. Instead, he grunted, "What?"

"You're mad at me."

"Not mad. Irritated."

Rowan settled Avery on the railing of the front porch and leaned her back against the house. "What did I do wrong?"

"Where did you and Ryder go last week?"

Rowan kicked a gnarled tree root that jutted up from the ground. "We went somewhere for Kane."

"Yeah, I figured, except Ryder's bound by some dumbass pinky swear and is avoiding the hell out of me, and I can't help but think the tension between me and my best friend is…"

"My fault," she finished quietly.

Weston sighed and leaned on the handle of the ax. "Roe, this was supposed to go differently. When you came for me and Avery at Raven's Hollow, I thought, fuck yes, finally she's out of the mountains and she can get over the shit that happened. Because you couldn't there. You were stuck. I saw it, your dad saw it, Damon saw it."

"I know."

"Do you?"

"Yeah, Wes! You think I was oblivious? You left. You drove away and started making your own life, and I was so jealous. I wanted to do that, too, but the thought of leaving was terrifying. It was easy on me to stay. Easy on my dragon. I saw the way everyone looked at me. I noticed the way they talked to me. Like I was weak. All the gentle nudging to go on vacation, to get out of the mountains, to find a job farther away. I fucking got it, okay? But I'm not like you. I'm not brave. I want to be, but I'm not there yet. You are at a totally different part of your journey than me, and sometimes I think you're too hard on me. And maybe you're too hard on me because you're being even harder on yourself in your head. Wes, what happened with Byron wasn't your fault. You warned me off him, and I didn't listen. That's on me. I never blamed you."

Wes wouldn't meet her eyes anymore, so she charged on because she knew she was right. "You fought every time someone came after Damon's Mountains. As soon as you were old enough, you went to battle every time, no questions, no fear. And I looked up to you. I wished I could be more like you because you were this raven, charging into battle, and I was this fucking dragon shaking in the shadows. I love you like my own flesh and blood brother, Wes, and I'm sorry I'm not stronger, but I'm trying."

"I can't sleep," he murmured. And when he looked at her, his raven-dark eyes were rimmed with moisture. "I keep visiting you in that goddamned cabin. I keep seeing Byron hit you for crying."

"Nooo, no, no, stop, Wes." Fuck, she didn't know he could see the past! "I don't want to talk about this."

"I have to, Roe! I don't know what else to do. It's playing on a loop." Weston threw his hat against the cabin and gripped the back of his neck. "I see you whispering to yourself at night when it was dark and your kidnappers were sleeping. You are begging your dragon to help you, and I didn't know it was like that. I was so pissed at you for hitting one obstacle in your life and slamming on the brakes, but it was awful for you. I see them beating you so you'll scream for Damon. I see them cutting your goddamn hand nearly off. I see Creed barreling through the wall and killing Byron, and I see the terror in your eyes, blood sprayed across your face. I hear you whimpering as you run from the house, the horror in your eyes as you look up, and you're glowing because Damon's fire is already coming and I'm standing right beside you screaming for you to run, but you can't hear me. And then I blink, and you're here, in Harper's Mountains, looking up at the sky with tears streaming down your face. You're older and you look so sad, just...destroyed. I know I'm going to lose you, and I can't fucking stop it. It's Byron all over again.

Whatever you're doing with Dark Kane, whatever is happening, you have to stop it. You have to save yourself."

"He wouldn't hurt me."

"You don't know that!"

"I do too, Wes!" She lifted her hair and showed him the claiming mark. "He picked me. I'm his mate. He can't hurt me because he loves me."

"He isn't like the rest of us."

"And being different is such a sin?" She was yelling now, angry. "You're telling me to let him go, but he is part of me now, Wes."

"You said that about Byron."

"Stop pinning the sins of my youth on the woman I have become. Kane makes me happy, Wes. Happy. Do you know how long I've waited to feel like this? You had to fight for Avery—"

"That's different."

"It's not. You all got to pick your mates. You got to fight for them." Rowan strode toward Wes and hugged his rigid body tight. She didn't even care if her skin burned him. She held on. "I fucking love you, Wes, but you aren't my keeper. I am. Whatever happens to me is on me. Not you, okay?" She dipped her voice to a whisper. "Let me love him. Be happy for me. I found my mate outside of Damon's Mountains, just like you always wanted. Let me be happy, Wes."

His arms went slowly to her back, and he sighed, rested his cheek against her hair. "I just want you to be okay."

"I will be." She'd infused steel into her voice because she believed it. Because she had to believe that Kane wouldn't hurt her when the time came.

It had been days since she'd found Ben and got the key to unlocking the cage of The Darkness, but she was a careful decision maker. She always had been. She was taking Ben's warning seriously, and Weston's, too. Wes thought she hadn't learned from her mistakes with Byron, but he was wrong.

With Weston's vision though, the decision was made.

If he saw fire, then fire was coming.

Someday, she was going to give Kane his dragon back, and she hoped like hell she would be ready for the flames.

EIGHTEEN

"Don't get frustrated with yourself," Alana said, waving her oven mitt in front of the billowing smoke that was rolling out of the oven. "You're still learning, and I'm not mad."

"I swear I thought I set the timer." But then again, she'd been mighty pre-occupied with thoughts of Kane all day, too, so it was a miracle this hadn't happened earlier.

The smoke alarm started going off as Alana pulled the blackened lemon pastries from the oven. They looked like rows of charcoal, and Rowan groaned. One of the unappetizing hunks lit on fire and fizzled in an instant. Alana dropped the pan on top of the counter with a clatter while Rowan jammed the handle of a broom up at the alarm until the ear-splitting noise faded to nothing.

Alana turned off the oven and locked eyes with Rowan. There was this loaded second before they burst out laughing. Thank God it was at the end of the day and no customers were in Alana's Coffee & Sweets right now.

Rowan pressed her hands against her blushing cheeks and scrunched up her face in apology. "Would you believe me if I told you I was actually decent at baking?"

Alana was wheezing with laughter. "No."

"Stop," Rowan said, swallowing her giggles. "What if I had done this during the breakfast rush?"

"I have a feeling you've learned your lesson." Alana picked up a hunk of burned pastry with a pair of tongs and shoved it toward Rowan. "You want to eat some ashes, dragon?"

"Ew, no. I'm not an ash-eater."

"Yeah, well, neither was Harper until someone threatened her mountains."

A pang of unexpected envy washed through Rowan. She would never have her own mountains to treasure. Instead, she'd picked a hunk of melted metal to covet.

She, Rowan Barnett, was the worst dragon in history.

The bell above the door up front dinged, and a familiar voice called out, "What smells so good?"

Alana snorted, and now Rowan's face was on fire because of course Kane would come in right when she'd burned the pastries. They'd been spending every minute they could together for a few weeks now. She bore his mark, but she still didn't want him changing his mind about her.

When she stepped into the main room, Kane stood with his back to the windows, a halo of light making his edges all saturated and blurry. He wore a light gray sweater that was so tight she could make out his chest in perfect definition. The top two buttons were undone, exposing the line between his pecs and a single, seductive curl of tattoo ink. He stood tall and strong, his sleeves rolled up to his elbows and a crooked smile on his face. He'd trimmed his beard short, and his hair was flipped to the left side today, exposing those old scars he'd gotten from Apex. He cared less lately about hiding them, and though she hadn't told him, she was proud of him for that.

"You look like sex on a stick," she said, leaning over the counter.

Kane bit his bottom lip and gave her a cocky grin. "You look pretty fuckin' delicious yourself, princess."

"I thought about something."

"Uh oh."

"Blackwing Dragon calling me princess, like I'm some damsel in distress."

The smile dipped from his lips, and he lowered his gravelly voice. "No Rowan. You're no damsel. You're the dragon clinging to the castle tower blowing fire. I'm the knight who wishes he had wings. I won't call you princess anymore. That's not what you are."

The seriousness of his tone surprised her. She'd thought they were joking. "Are you okay?"

"Yeah." He bumped his fist against the counter a few times. "I came to ask you out."

"Another date?" she asked excitedly. He'd been taking really good care of her, taking her out, showing her the town. She was pretty certain he was trying to get her to fall in love with his territory, and it was definitely working.

"Kind of? I came to ask Alana out, too."

Rowan growled deep in her chest, and Kane huffed a laugh. "Easy dragon. I'm inviting all the Bloodrunners. The others are already en route."

"En route to where?" Alana asked, resting her elbows on the counter right beside Rowan.

Kane tipped his chin up and grinned down at them. "Maybe I have plans for us tonight."

"Wait, *us* like the whole crew?" Rowan asked excitedly.

"Yeah, I got sick of saying no to Ryder's bro-date invites and—" Kane made an *oof* sound when Rowan launched herself over the counter and into his arms.

He chuckled deep and warm against her ear and held her, rocked her slightly like he'd missed her. God, she loved him so much. Loved the changes she'd seen in him over the last few weeks. Little by little, he was opening himself up to the crew, and maybe it started out because he wanted to make her happy. But somewhere along the way, his smiles had become easier with the Bloodrunners. His jokes had loosened up, he had stopped flinching when they touched him, and he didn't even say the F-word when Ryder hugged him goodbye anymore. And twice in the last week, he'd shown up in Harper's Mountains unannounced and had dinner with the crew just because he seemed to want to be near Rowan, but also the Bloodrunners. And now this?

"I'm so proud of you," she whispered.

"You don't even know what I have planned."

"Not about that, silly monster. I mean, I'm proud of you for opening up."

"I don't want to hold you back. I want to give you things, not take them away."

He eased her back and cupped her neck, his thumb on her pulse as he pressed his lips to hers. This wasn't one of the hard, desperate kisses they'd shared so often. This one was soft. It was swaying like slow-dance music and lips that fit perfectly together. It was holding for a few seconds, then easing away with a sweet smack. It was a lingering smile on his lips that stunned her.

"Come on, ladies," he said with a grin. "The crew is waiting. Lock up, and I'll be in the truck."

Ten minutes later, Rowan and Alana piled in Kane's Bronco. And then it was music blaring, windows down, wind in their hair as they sang along and made their hands do waves in the open air. Kane kept looking at her and Alana with an amused smile, so different from the moody Kane she'd met in the airport those weeks ago.

Kane wore his sunglasses, but as soon as he pulled into the River's Edge restaurant parking lot, he left them in a cup holder with Rowan's. He wasn't hiding his eyes today. The sunglasses had been for function only, to shield him from the sunlight.

"Early dinner?" Rowan asked as Kane limped up behind her.

He slid his arms over her chest, then pointed to the river behind the restaurant. On the opposite bank was a big raft, the Bloodrunners standing around it and talking to a man who was handing out lifejackets.

"Are we rafting?" Alana asked excitedly.

"We are," Kane said with a chuckle.

Aaron, the blond-haired giant, was down below with the others, but the second Alana spoke, his eyes went straight to her. When he beamed a greeting smile at her, Alana squealed and jogged for the bridge that would get her to her mate.

Rowan walked backward, holding Kane's hands. "Do we look all lovey and gross like them?"

"Probably. Not my fault. Yours."

"You like it," she accused, slipping her hand against his elbow. "I thought you couldn't get your leg wet."

"I'm wearing the right one today."

"Fuckin' sexy," she muttered, grabbing his firm butt.

With a snarl, Kane clamped his teeth onto her neck, bit down gently, sucked hard enough to leave a mark, then released her. She wouldn't admit it, but every time he did that, she wanted to go all submissive and still. She wanted to open her legs for him and pull his hand between her thighs, but Kane didn't need to go around thinking she had the instincts of a submissive. He'd just stopped calling her princess after all.

They crossed the bridge and made their way down the pebble beach to the others. Rowan practically glowed when Kane clapped hands with Ryder mannishly and pulled him in for a rough hug, then turned and did the same with Aaron and Wyatt.

He hesitated for a moment with Wes, but the Novak Raven held out his hand and did the same. Gaze averted, Weston muttered, "This is good, man."

"Thanks," Kane murmured before turning to take

his life vest from the outstretched hand of an instructor. "Hey, Mike."

Mike said, "Long time no see. You sure you have them, or do you want me to assist?"

Rowan frowned. "What do you mean?"

Mike swatted at Kane's chest, but missed because he flinched away. "This guy was our best raft guide for about three months before Martin stole him away from us. You're in good hands, but still…" He handed Alana and Rowan waivers. "Sign these in case you die."

Rowan gulped. "Wait, how dangerous is this?"

"Tourists do this every day, and with no experience," Kane said with a teasing smile. "Don't make me start calling you princess again."

She narrowed her eyes at him, then scribbled her name across the bottom and called, "shotgun."

"There is no shotgun," Ryder said, buckling his life jacket. "Or else I would've called it already. Is there food? I'm hungry."

Lexi swatted his ass. "Baby, you're always hungry."

"For pussy."

"Ryder," Harper and Avery both groaned.

Rowan put her hair into a ponytail as Kane buckled her vest. "There's food at the end. Have you been to Gordy's Pizza Shack yet? We'll pull up on the bank and Mike will give us a ride back here when we're done eating."

"That's nice of you, Mike!" Ryder called after the retreating man.

"I'm getting paid," Mike called over his shoulder.

"I've lived around here all my life and never done tourist excursions," Alana said in an excited voice. She was having to loosen the straps of her life vest to accommodate her big boobs. They were currently all shoved up to her chin, and Aaron was staring. "Wait," Alana said with a frown at the rapids, "the water is really cold this time of year."

Weston stooped and scooped water, then splashed it at Alana, who danced out of the way. "Then don't fall in, Keller!"

"And don't push me in, Novak," Alana said, jamming her finger at him. Her scarred lip curved up in a smile. "P. S. I really liked that you just called me by my new last name."

Aaron hugged her from behind and nuzzled her neck. "Sounds good on you, baby."

"Barf!" Ryder yelled.

It was then that Rowan noticed his clothes. "Ryder Croy, why the hell are you wearing cut-off shorts?"

"Because Lexi likes them." When he shoved the raft into the shallows, his muscled-up butt cheeks hung out the bottom. Rowan was pretty sure she saw the outline of his chode. Everyone moaned in unison except for Lexi, who was doubled over with her arms around her stomach cracking up.

Rowan pulled her phone out quick and snapped a picture of his shorts and knee-high gym socks.

"What are you doing?" Kane asked.

"I'm gonna send this little gem to a Boarlander named Clinton."

"You should," Ryder said, settling the raft into the thigh high water. "He'll love me even more. Get in, crew, I want pizza." He held out his hand for Lexi and helped her in like she was his queen.

Kane took the back to instruct them, so Rowan settled on the edge of the inflated raft right in front of him and wedged her tennis shoes under a flap to keep her balance. She picked up one of the paddles from the floorboard as the raft bumped and bounced with everyone getting settled.

A splash of freezing water soaked her shirt, and she gasped at the shock of it. Slowly, she turned, and Kane was wearing the biggest, unapologetic grin she'd ever seen in her life. "You're gonna get wet, Roe. Now you won't be surprised by it."

"Monster," she whispered.

His sexy dragon eyes flashed with intensity in the instant before his lips pressed against hers, warming her from the inside out. Kane was a really hard man to stay mad at.

Ryder jumped in, and they were off, Kane directing them from the back. They were clumsy at first, paddling all wrong and laughing too damn much. Once they got turned around backward and Ryder nearly flipped the raft with his desperation to switch seats with Aaron. Apparently the front passenger got the wettest.

Weston was sitting in front of Rowan, and after the third time of him slapping the back of his neck, he twisted in his seat and glared at Kane. "Do you mind, man?"

"What?" Kane asked, sounding baffled.

But Weston had a point. There was a low

humming noise coming from him, and the air felt heavier the farther into the rapids they got.

Rowan rubbed the standing hairs on her own neck. "Are you worked up?"

Kane looked utterly confused. "I'm fine." After a few minutes of concentrating on the rapids and not crashing into rocks, the weight lifted, and Weston stopped with the dirty looks.

Rowan wondered if he even realized how present The Darkness was, or if he'd just gotten used to the rumbling and the dominance. Or perhaps he was in denial. But the more time Rowan spent with him, the more she could feel his inner dragon. He wasn't even sleeping or locked away as she'd first thought when she found out about the cleansing. He was just...waiting.

Rowan glanced over at Harper who was sitting across the raft, but she didn't seem to notice anything threatening. She wore a beatific smile as she paddled, water splashing on her side of the boat, her dark hair wet from the rapids. Her growing belly pushed against her life jacket, and for a moment, Rowan was stunned with how happy she looked. Wyatt sat in front of her. He turned just then and smiled at his mate easily. They'd been ripped up when they'd split at age eighteen, and now look at them. Wyatt, the one who was supposed to be this great grizzly alpha, was supporting Harper as she ran the Bloodrunners.

Ryder was happily chirping up front next to Lexi, and Weston's touch never strayed far from Avery. Alana and Aaron were so freaking cute, and Rowan was proud. She was happy for her friends and what they'd found here. She was happy she'd left Damon's Mountains because it had gotten her here, to this beautiful moment. Kane rested his leg against hers as if he could sense her swinging emotions, and she rested her hand on his knee. It was his bad one, the one that hurt him, but he didn't grimace when she got too close to it anymore. Instead, he leaned in closer and winked at her as he told the crew to bank to the right so they could head to the restaurant that lumbered on the edge of the river up ahead.

Rowan's heart fluttered with happiness. One hour of riding the river amid the happy chattering and teamwork of the Bloodrunners, and she was filled with a charge of energy. It was joy, she realized. Had she ever felt that before?

Kane and the boys pulled the raft up onto the

sand, and Harper draped her arm over Rowan's shoulders. "I'm glad you're here," she murmured, her bi-colored eyes on the others as they secured the raft. "I've never seen Kane like this. You're good for him, Roe."

Rowan draped her arms gently around Harper's slightly rounded waist and watched Kane laugh at something pervy that Ryder said. "You really think so?"

"I know so." Harper strode off behind the others toward the pizza shack. She turned and walked a few steps backward. "You're good for the Bloodrunners too, you know." She arched her dark eyebrows and turned back around to join Wyatt.

Kane was waiting for her, jeans splattered with water, shirt plastered to his abdominals, eyes glowing in the dark. Behind him, the lightning bugs were putting on a show in the woods.

She was drawn to him like she had no control over her body at all. It was as if they were both holding the ends of a strip of rubber, and the only thing that eased the tension was being close to him. Was this what it was like for the Bloodrunners and their mates? Was this what it was like for her parents?

Rowan slipped her arms around his waist, but Kane stooped slightly and picked her up. When she wrapped her legs around his hips, he nipped her bottom lip and then rested his cheek against hers. "Roe?"

She hugged his neck and leaned into his words. "Yeah?"

His whisper was so soft, so quiet, she would've missed it if she wasn't so close to him. "I love you."

The prickling tears in her eyes were instant. It was just them on the beach, surrounded by the drone of insects and the twinkling lights of the fireflies. She closed her eyes and just felt him. Absorbed his warmth and his strength. She made sure her voice would be steady before she parted her lips and said on a breath, "I love you back."

"Pizza!" Ryder yelled from the back door of the hole-in-the-wall restaurant. "Plus it's time for you to open your birthday gift."

"It's not my birthday," Kane said.

"It is according to your social media accounts I made for you." Ryder looked at his phone. "You have four-hundred-thirty-seven happy birthday notifications."

Kane's defeated sigh drew a giggle from Rowan.

He settled her on her feet and rested his fingertips gently against her lower back. He still felt like a dominant titan beside her, but Kane would never hurt her. He would never ask her to submit, so what was the point of angling her face and exposing her neck like her instincts told her to do? She was his equal.

As Kane reached him, Ryder handed him a small wad of newspaper. Carefully, Kane pulled the paper off. It was a keychain.

"Happy pretend birthday, fourth best friend. I got your favorite color."

Kane's expression was unreadable as he stared down at the shiny black bear-paw beer bottle opener in his giant palm. "Thanks, man," he murmured, and now Rowan was gonna cry all over again.

Ryder scrunched up his face at her. "Gross, girl tears." And then he disappeared inside.

Kane hooked his present on his keychain, then shoved it in his back pocket, avoiding the hell out of her gaze, but she wasn't fooled. He felt…happy. Flattered, perhaps. He sure didn't feel overwhelming and heavy anymore.

She pulled his knuckles to her lips and then led him inside where the others had secured a big table on the open back deck. Beers were ordered, water for Harper, pizzas chosen, and the happy chatter picked up to a constant ebb and flow of sarcastic remarks, dirty jokes, and laughter. Kane was quiet, leaned back in his chair listening and chuckling with the others almost as if he couldn't believe he was here in this moment either. And when those gorgeous dragon greens landed on her, Rowan slid off her chair and into his lap where he rubbed her back gently and pressed his lips to the tip of her shoulder.

And this was one of those days—one she would always remember. A day when she'd had a jump in personal growth as she'd watched the same in the man she loved. A day when she realized happiness had taken over her life. A day when she hadn't thought about Byron or her many mistakes. A day when she hadn't pined for the mountains she'd left behind or obsessed about whether her treasure was safe in 1010 or not.

It was the day she stopped being the princess in the tower, and became the dragon instead.

NINETEEN

"Kane the raft guide," Aaron said from the back seat where he had his arm around Alana's shoulders and his other hand resting out the open window. "Where else have you worked?"

Kane slid his hand over Rowan's thigh comfortably and turned onto the dirt road that led to Harper's Mountains. "I was a surf instructor for a few months out in California when I was twenty."

"Badass. Why did you move here?"

Kane's hand tightened around her leg. "Army had me for a few years."

"You volunteered?" Aaron sounded surprised. Rowan glanced over her shoulder at him and Alana's mouths hanging open. The Bloodrunners didn't seem to know a whole hell of a lot about Kane.

"Drafted was more like it, and afterward, the leg didn't work so well, so I moved around a lot. Picked up work where I could. I had trouble settling territory because anywhere that was attractive to me was already claimed by a crew, sometimes two or three. I landed here a few years back and only had the vamps and Wyatt to hold off until the rest of the crew started showing up. I thought I was done when Harper waltzed into Dratz that first night. Thought for sure I would have to move on like all the other times, but she never pushed me out. None of you did. I waited, but you didn't seem that interested."

"Yeah, that's not really how any of us were raised," Aaron said. "Most of the crew lived in Damon's Mountains in close proximity to other shifters. I lived in a big crew and spent summers there. Having a shit-ton of shifters around is natural if you're raised that way. I never even thought about pushing you out. I haven't heard any of the other Bloodrunners mention it either. The vamps, though…" Aaron rubbed the scars on his neck and stared out the window. "The vamps and the wolves needed to go."

Kane pulled through the gate of Harper's Mountains. "I wasn't sad to see them scatter. I had the coven and the pack both breathing down my neck. If the Bloodrunners lost that territory dispute, I would've had to run again. I was rooting for you not to die."

Aaron snorted. "Thanks, man."

The others were piling out of Weston's truck, and the Novak Raven himself approached Kane. "We're gonna Change together tonight." Wes cleared his throat and shoved his hands in his pockets. "Wanted to know if you want to Change with us, too."

Kane froze. "Me?"

"Yeah, Blackwing, you're special to Rowan, and she hasn't been Changing lately for whatever stupid reason, and after tonight…well…it'll be good for everyone. It'll be fun. A good way to end the night."

Kane's chest was heaving with his breath, so Rowan slipped her hand around his stony bicep. Kane flinched. "It wouldn't be a good way to end the night for me."

"What?" Weston looked around at the gathering Bloodrunners. "This is the fucking olive branch. Take it."

"Wes, he's good, man," Ryder said low. "Kane's probably tired. Been a big day hanging out with us."

Okay, so her suspicions were true then. No one knew Kane didn't have his dragon. No one but her, Ryder thanks to the trip to visit Ben, and maybe Wyatt from the unsurprised look on his face.

"I can't shift, Novak," Kane said in a dark voice. "And why haven't you been shifting?" he asked Rowan.

"I haven't felt like it," she lied.

"Bullshit. Is it guilt?"

Rowan hunched under the anger in his voice.

"I don't understand," Harper said. "Why can't you Change?"

"Because I don't have a fucking dragon to Change into. Roe, you're gonna make yourself sick."

"Harper hasn't been Changing lately either," Rowan argued.

"Because she's pregnant. You have no reason not to give your dragon time."

"Yeah, well every time I Change now I feel sad, Kane."

"Why?" he barked out.

"Because I want to Change with you! It doesn't

feel right having a dragon and flying around all willy-nilly happy when you can't do the same. It's not fair."

"What the fuck is going on?" Weston asked. "Kane, you have fucking dragon eyes and you feel like a monster." He held his hands out and looked around. "Can you all not feel that? I'm calling bullshit on you not having a dragon. I can barely breathe right now, and you're snarling."

Indeed he was, and the noise was terrifying.

"Dude," Ryder said gently, pushing on Weston's chest to keep him in place. "You know what my real dad wanted to do to me?" He tipped his head at Kane. "That happened to him. Cut him a break, okay?"

The anger and confusion washed away from Weston in an instant. It was replaced by the pallid complexion of a man who might get sick. "Holy shit," he murmured.

Avery strode forward, her eyes on the ground, her fists clenched at her side. The timid little raven shifter was shaking like a leaf, but she didn't stop until she was wrapped around Kane's waist, hugging him. "I'm sorry," she said thickly.

"I'm fine," Kane said in an empty voice. "It happened a long time ago."

Harper's face fell and she turned away, but not before Rowan saw a tear stream down her cheek. Her shoulders shook, and she had a hand over her mouth as though she was trying to stifle her crying. Wyatt hugged her, murmuring something too low for Rowan to hear.

And Rowan understood such an emotional response. She hadn't always gotten along with her dragon, or even trusted her, but the idea of a huge piece of her being stripped out of her, of never feeling the wind on her scales again, was unfathomable.

Any shifter here could empathize, and from the tears in Lexi's eyes, even the human could, too. "You can stay with me and Harper while they Change," Lexi said in a weak, shaky voice. "I know it's not the same, but—"

"I'm good. I think I'm gonna call it a night." Kane scrubbed his hands down his face roughly and dislodged himself from Rowan and Avery's grasp. "Have a nice Change," he murmured hoarsely before he climbed into his Bronco and peeled out of Harper's Mountains.

"Oh, my God," Alana whispered. "Kane's been cleansed?"

"Is there anything that can be done for him?" Avery sobbed.

Ryder had squatted down in the grass, stripping a branch of its leaves as he watched the taillights of Kane's ride fade away. He dragged his blazing gold eyes up to Rowan and arched his ruddy eyebrows in question.

She'd waffled tonight on whether she was going to bite him or not. Why? Because Kane had been happy. At least he'd seemed to be, and she'd thought for a moment she could let his dragon sleep and he would be okay. She'd thought maybe Weston's vision could be changed and that Kane could just go on like he was. But his pain had leaked out here, and now she was more confused than ever.

Love will bring on the End of Days.
The End of Days.

Was there anything that could be done? Maybe, but at what cost to Kane? At what cost to the world?

Softly, Rowan whispered, "I don't know."

****

Kane couldn't breathe. His chest felt as if a bus had parked on top of his ribcage.

He couldn't stop the deep rumbling there

anymore, and his knuckles had turned white from his grip on the steering wheel.

He'd planned on keeping the secret until the day he died, but Rowan had come in and changed everything. She'd made him open up, yes, but being with her also put him in the path of the crew. He'd lost the balance that had kept him steady all these years.

Stay on the outside where he belonged, and he could make it one day at a time.

But he'd seen the pity in the Bloodrunners' eyes when they'd found out about the cleansing. He'd seen the tears and the horror. The disgust. And even if those arrows of pity weren't aimed at him, it hurt like his heart had been pierced.

Outsider. Freak.

Kane slammed on the brakes of his Bronco and banked his open palm against the steering wheel over and over until the steering column bent backward. Fucking dragon strength. What good had that done him?

Kane stumbled out of his ride and inside the cabin.

Heightened strength had got him recruited into

war. It had put him on special forces. It had put him in the dark, moving through enemy lines like the ghost he was. His strength had stayed, but his healing had not, and now his fucking leg hurt so bad. How many nights had he wanted to disappear into a bottle of whiskey just to numb the pain? How many nights had he lay on the floor, staring at the ceiling, remembering what it felt like to fly? To feel powerful? To feel in control? To breathe fucking fire?

He hit the cold water in the shower and stumbled in, clothes still on, just to ease the flames lapping his skin. He was burning from the inside out. Yearning from the inside out.

Where the fuck are you?

He locked his arms against the shower, and his muscles twitched and jumped, making it hard to stay steady.

Rowan had been avoiding her Changes. She'd felt guilty because of him, and that's the last thing he wanted. A part of him wanted to see her dragon so fucking bad he couldn't stand it. And then there was the weak part. The dark part that didn't want to ever see her Change because he knew the outcome of that. He wouldn't be able to pretend anymore. He wouldn't be able to act like he was worthy of her. Like he was a good match. He was a fucking human in a world of shifters, and she was born to cling to mountains and roar fire at anyone who threatened her.

And what could he do? He could watch her and wish he was like her.

Where the fuck are you?

The water wasn't helping. He had something inside of him that was pulsing and filling him with rage. Filling him with something he didn't understand.

Gasping for air, Kane ripped his soaking shirt from his body and stumbled through the house until he felt the cool wind outside. He limped into the clearing in front of his lair. Pain, pain, pain. Pain on the outside, pain on the inside, and he was drowning. He would never escape the darkness, but The Darkness had escaped him. He had been rendered empty. And that emptiness was filling with black fog that would be the death of him and the heartbreak of his beautiful Rowan.

There was a reason she refused to bite him when they were together. He didn't deserve her claiming mark. He knew it, and Rowan knew it, too.

If he'd been strong enough to keep his dragon—to control him, to save him—he could've kept Rowan for always. He could've kept his treasure safe and happy. He could've given her smiles forever, but instead, there would be nights like this when her lip would tremble and her eyes would fill with tears, and she would feel bad for what she was because he hadn't been strong enough.

Kane fell to his knees, eyes burning, chest burning, arms burning.

He looked up at the sky, breaking apart on the inside, wishing to God he could break apart on the outside and fly. He clenched his fists and screamed, "Where the fuck are you?"

TWENTY

Lightning flashed behind the Smoky Mountains, and storm clouds roiled in the sky, making the evening look darker, more sinister. A fitting mood for the apocalypse because Rowan had made up her mind now.

She pushed against her heel, rocking the chair under her.

She'd Changed and flown to Kane's cabin last night. And then naked and human, she'd stood shielded by the thick forest. She'd watched him fall to his knees and scream at the sky, every muscle tensed, fists out and clenched, yelling, "Where the fuck are you?"

Oh, Kane had been hiding deep pain from her. In

that moment, his agony had pulsed against her body and made her dry heave into the ivy.

There was no more wavering anymore. The time had come to decide—is he strong enough or not? *Am I?*

The answer had to be yes because she couldn't stand this awful poisonous feeling in her chest anymore. She loved Kane with every fiber of her being, and her withholding freedom for his dragon was hurting him. It would always hurt him.

Bite him. Free him.

Another flash of lightning, and a deep roll of thunder sounded. Rowan blinked slowly and lifted her gaze to the giant snowy owl who stood watching her from the thick branches of a pine. It was as if Ryder could tell what she was thinking. As if he could read her thoughts and see the fire coming. His feathers were ruffled, his gold eyes trained on her, unblinking.

She'd been recruited to protect the Bloodrunners, and she would at any cost.

Any cost other than her mate's happiness.

Air Ryder turned his head slowly toward the gate, and she could hear it too—the rumble of a late-model Bronco engine.

He can do this. Set him free.

Rowan stood and leaned on the railing of the porch as Kane stepped from his ride. He wasn't meeting her eyes today, but last night had been rough. She understood. He wore black. A black T-shirt over dark jeans and black work boots. Black sunglasses to match his black hair that hung in a wave in front of his face.

Trust him.

Lightning streaked the sky, closer this time. Kane didn't hunch under the booming sound it created. He stopped at the bottom stair, his hands clenched at his sides, his tattoos stark against the pale skin of his left arm. Roses and skulls. Beauty and death.

"We need to talk," he said in a gruff voice.

"You aren't leaving me," she said sternly.

"You have a dragon you don't want, and I want a dragon I can never have. We aren't the same. I think it's best if I make a life outside of the Smoky—"

"You aren't giving me a day like yesterday and then taking that away from me, Kane."

"Dark Kane."

"Stop it. You marked me, you chose me, you

drew my heart from Damon's Mountains to yours, so for better or worse, we're in this." She tilted her chin higher and inhaled a deep, steadying breath. "I have to show you something."

"If it's your treasure, I've already seen it."

Rowan frowned. "What?"

"I looked when you were asleep a couple weeks ago. Metal." His lip snarled up, and he smelled of anger. "You think metal is your treasure."

"I don't think, Kane. *I know*. I obsess about it. I feel attached to it. It kept me safe."

"And I can't." Kane cocked his head, exposed his neck. "If I go far enough away—"

"I'll follow—"

"If I give you space, you can find a better match."

"And what about you?"

He shrugged a shoulder up and let it fall again.

"Will you find a better match than me, Kane?" she asked louder, not about to let him ignore his way out of this one.

"No! Okay? You're it. If I was like you, a shifter, a dragon, you would be my treasure."

She gasped and held onto the porch railing to steady herself. Her voice would tremble if she spoke, and she needed to be strong right now, so she swallowed hard and blew out a shaking breath before she responded. "You are my match, Kane. You are. No one else gets me like you. No one else has even tried. Things are going to change today. In here. In 1010, things will be different. And I'm scared, and I don't know what is going to happen, and I can't keep my head on straight if I have to think about you leaving me. Please."

When Kane took his glasses off, his eyes were so sad. "You would settle for a broken man?"

"You won't stay broken."

"You can't fix me, Roe."

He was wrong, though. She was going to give him the biggest gift her love could give him. "Come inside," she murmured. Rowan turned on her heel and pushed open the door, then stepped into 1010.

She'd thought about doing this in his mountains, but Weston swore this place had magic, and she needed it right now. She needed it to make her braver. She needed it to make this easier on Kane, easier on The Darkness.

God, let Ben be right. Let this work.

Kane's boots echoed across the floorboards, and

the door clicked quietly closed behind him. Outside, the thunder rolled, but in here, it was so quiet the air charged with electricity between them. The lights were off, and Kane's eyes glowed green as he shifted his weight side to side like some predator watching his prey. She wasn't the prey, though. Not today. She was the hunter.

"I asked you once, if you could, would you have your dragon back?"

Kane ticked an irritated sound and hooked his hands on his hips.

"You didn't answer then," she pushed on. "I need you to answer now."

After a few seconds of stalling, he gritted out, "Yeah, Roe. I wish I was strong enough to still have the dragon."

Rowan hesitated for a moment, then pulled her shirt over her head and dropped it to the floor.

"What are you doing?" Kane asked, glowing eyes glued to her breasts as she unsnapped her bra.

She was scared. Shaking. This was a big moment. Her road had been forked, and this was her choosing the path surrounded by dark woods. It was the path most unclear, but Kane was worth the risk. He was worth everything.

"Touch me," she whispered, the tension in her chest tight.

Kane strode toward her like a trail of gunpowder on the ground, and the second he swept her up in his arms, heat exploded between them. He rammed her backward until the backs of her knees hit the kitchen table. His lips were hard and unforgiving. This was the desperate kiss that came after a near-loss. It was the kiss that followed near-death experiences, and that's what he'd almost done to both of them. He'd come here in hopes of breaking their bond. Fuck. No.

She bit him hard enough to draw blood from his lip, and a feral snarl ratcheted up his throat. He gripped her hair hard and trailed sucking kisses down her neck as he unfastened his pants with his other hand. Rowan clawed her fingers, dug into his back, pulled him closer. The table under her scooted loudly across the floor as Kane jammed them back by inches.

There was a loud *riiip*, and her shorts were in tatters. Her panties, too. Kane's lips were back on hers, and he grunted a wild sound as his fingers dug into her hips. When he pulled her forward, slid into her, Rowan arched against him and cried out. She fucking loved him like this—barely in control, snarling, out of his mind with lust for her. And she could feel The Darkness. So seductively, he was calling out to her. Reaching out to her, but he didn't feel scary.

He felt like home.

Kane won't hurt us.

Kane dragged her to the very edge of the table and slammed into her over and over, his body moving like crashing waves against her, his dick so long, so thick, filling her just right.

He pushed her backward, climbed onto the table, spread her legs with his good knee, and bucked into her even deeper, his body tensing with every stroke inside her, his abs hard against her stomach. When he lowered his lips to her breast and sucked her nipple hard, she sank her claws into the back of his neck and dragged him closer in desperation. She was losing her mind, seeing him in shades of red like a heat signature.

Bite him!

His eyes were so bright when he locked gazes with her, so inhuman. He bared his teeth and rested his forehead against hers as she came. Her orgasm was explosive and took up her whole mind as she pressed her lips against his chest, right over his heart.

As he slammed into her faster, she bit him gently, testing.

"Do it," he begged.

Kane pushed deeply into her and gripped the back of her neck, cradled her against him as the first shot of warmth flooded her middle. "Fuck, Rowan, do it!"

Rowan bit down as hard as she could. She bit until her mouth flooded with iron, until he yelled her name. Until her belly was full of his seed and he wasn't begging her anymore.

She bit down until she could feel the long, low snarl of The Darkness vibrate from Kane's body and fill the air.

She released his tattered skin, and Kane froze above her, eyes sparking like green fire. His elongated pupils constricted until he looked like a snake ready to strike. His chest dripped a steady stream of crimson onto her, and the terrifying sound emanating from him was louder. The blood suddenly tapered to a drip, and then nothing at all. Kane looked down in horror at the claiming mark that was already sealing up.

It was working.

Kane launched off her, gripping his chest as though it was burning. His face contorted with pain. "What did you do?"

"I set you free."

"Rowan," he said, chest heaving. "You didn't set me free. You killed us all."

His body pulsed, became bigger, and then constricted again. Kane threw open the door and shielded his eyes from the daylight.

"It's okay, Kane," she said, trailing him to the front yard.

The Bloodrunners were gathered, as if The Darkness had called them from their cabins. None of them looked surprised or confused. Their pupils were blown, and they looked somber. Harper stood in front of them, chin up, looking down at Kane where he fell to his knees in the dirt.

Kane grabbed his head and screamed a bloodcurdling, pained sound.

"Fighting him won't do any good," Weston said.

Kane's skin on his back was cracking like

cement, then healing, then cracking again. Roe didn't understand. This isn't how a Change should be!

She bolted for him, hugged him, but he turned his attention on Wyatt. "Get Harper out of here."

"Kane," Wyatt said, hands out, pleading.

"If you want your mate to live, hide her deep underground. Now!" Kane's voice was that of a beast.

Wyatt ushered Harper toward his truck, and the girls followed.

Aaron peeled off his shirt as if readying to Change for battle, but Rowan cut him off. "Run, Aaron. All of you, get out of here."

Aaron and Ryder's eyes were wide with fear as Kane's form grew and shrank again. They peeled off, hopped in the back of Wyatt's truck, and then it was just Rowan and Wes, watching the Bloodrunners speed away, spraying gravel and kicking up plumes of dust in their wake.

"Wes, go!"

"I can't leave you."

"Please!"

"Dammit, I can't leave you, Roe! I've watched this. I've watched it, and I can't leave."

Oh, she knew what he meant. Death was coming

for her, and he didn't want her to do this alone.

Kane screamed again, his body cracking and healing, pulsing. His voice built to a horrifying roar that shook the woods. Blood was streaming from his eyes. He couldn't buy Wes much more time.

She bolted for the Novak Raven, cupped his cheeks hard. "You'll leave me because this is my choice. I've got this."

"You don't." Wes looked devastated, but screw what he'd seen. Power throbbed within her. Dragon wanted out. She was ready for war. Ready to protect Kane, ready to protect the world.

"Take care of Avery, Wes. That's what I want. Make her happy. Take care of Harper and the crew. *Live*," she gritted out, then shoved him away.

Weston shook his head, backing away slowly.

Kane slammed his fists on the ground, and two deep cracks blasted through the earth. "Leave us!" he bellowed as lighting flashed behind 1010.

And Weston was gone. He blurred into a massive raven, flew away, and didn't look back.

"Roe, Roe, Roe," Kane chanted, as though he was trying to use her name as an anchor to himself. When he looked up at her, his eyes were flashing brown, green, brown, green, and his face was contorted into something fearsome. "I'm sorry," he choked out right before his eyes turned green and held. A cruel smile twisted his lips, and he hunched inward.

Rowan sprinted out of the way as a massive, pitch black dragon exploded from Kane's body, growing and growing until it blocked out the sky. She skidded to a stop as The Darkness unfurled his long neck, lifted his spiked, armored face to the sky, and roared a deafening sound. He pushed up on powerful legs, his injured back one not seeming to hinder him at all. Long claws dug into earth, and his long tail curved around the edge of the woods. His wings looked strange. They were like the wet wings of a butterfly that had just emerged from the cocoon. But with a groan, The Darkness forced his wings open until they stretched across the tree canopy on either side of 1010.

Rowan stood frozen in fear. Frozen in awe. His wings weren't smooth and graceful like hers, but were riddled with holes and folded like a bat's wings. Lethal spikes protruded along the ridges of his wings. They were the color of night and monstrous. His pitch black scales were scarred and marred, as though he'd done centuries of battle, and his size…

Kane was bigger than Rowan, and bigger than Damon.

The last Blackwing Dragon was the largest living being on earth.

The true End of Days.

Fear snaked in her gut as The Darkness dragged a narrowed gaze to her. Two echoing clicks of his firestarter sounded, and The Darkness blasted into the air, cracking the ground around her feet, causing an earthquake that dumped her backward.

The first beat of his wings flattened her against the ground and stole her breath, and the second was even more powerful. He took to the sky, tucking his clawed feet close to his massive belly scales.

And then to her horror, he rained fire down onto the Smoky Mountains.

"No," she murmured as she stood and tracked his wide circle. She'd been wrong. Kane couldn't control the beast. No one could.

Smoke billowed from Harper's Mountains, and as he sprayed another stream of fire, and another, a sob left Rowan's throat. She'd done this. She'd breathed life into this monster.

The Darkness circled back around and headed straight for her. Rowan backed up to the tree line and stumbled on a root, fell hard on her back, and stared up in horror, tears streaming down her face as The Darkness positioned himself over 1010.

He opened his massive jaws, exposing a row of razor sharp teeth, and unleashed a spray of fire and lava onto the beloved cabin.

No, not onto the cabin. Onto her treasure.

"Kane, no!" she shrieked, running for 1010.

One. Two. Three seconds of Damon's dragon fire had almost melted the metal of her treasure all the way through. Four. Five.

Tears streamed down her cheeks as The Darkness destroyed her treasure. As he destroyed her.

Death. This is what Weston had seen—the intentional destruction of her treasure by the man she loved.

Rage rocketed through her body as The Darkness halted his fire, beat his wings in the air, and hovered there, watching her with his lips curled back in a soulless dragon's smile.

He'd killed her. She would get The Sickening and

die, and there was nothing that could save her now. The betrayal was too much.

Rowan screamed his name. "Kane!" And then let her dragon have her body.

She'd never Changed out of anger before, but power pounded through her as she beat her wings against the air currents.

He'd taken 1010, her comfort, her life. He'd taken everything, and for what? She'd freed him! She'd played into his hand perfectly. She'd listened to her dragon for the first time since Byron, and now look. Dragon had gotten her killed.

Rowan slammed into The Darkness's body and jammed her claws through his scales violently. Spew fire onto Harper's Mountains, put her friends in danger, and destroy her treasure? She was going to hurt him.

Rowan's dark silver dragon was smaller, but she was fueled with undiluted rage. She spun them around, beating her wings furiously, pulling them higher into the air as she sprayed a stream of fire across his throat. The Darkness roared in pain and tried to push her off, but she had dug her claws deep into him. He snapped at her face, but she dodged his bites. His Firestarter clicked, but he didn't rain lava on her. It was the only thing that could really hurt her in this form—dragon's fire, and he was withholding his, whatever that meant.

She didn't feel so charitable.

The storm clouds prickled her skin with millions of tiny drops of water as they drove upward through the storm, and now The Darkness was pushing her harder, flapping his demon wings, trying to escape.

The fucking End of Days. *Rowan* was the End of Days. The end of his days.

When he spun them in a barrel roll, she couldn't keep them up anymore, not like this. She pounded her wings desperately, but the earth was coming. She bit at his armor and blew balls of fire at him, but that didn't stop gravity. That didn't stop them from toppling to earth like two atom bombs.

At the last second, The Darkness twisted them hard and slammed to earth first, his back shattering the trees and the ground, shaking the mountains. Why had he done that? Why had he sacrificed himself for her comfort?

Her wind was knocked out of her, but she slid off him, circled around as he righted himself, both crushing trees beneath their feet. As soon as she could draw breath, she opened her mouth and roared her challenge at him. He might have saved her from pain, but he'd still killed her. Still burned her treasure. Still smiled like he was fucking amused by her oncoming slow death.

The Darkness stood and shook his massive, spiked head. He let off a short, barking roar, then another and another.

Rowan's heart beat so hard in her chest. She wanted to answer him. It was an apology. It was a call to arms. It was an invitation for her to join him in burning the land. Fuck his invitations.

Rowan clicked her Firestarter and pushed gas out of her lungs, sprayed his ribs with fire and charged. The Darkness caught her, latched his teeth onto her shoulder as they rolled over and over, felling forest under them. Rowan clamped her teeth onto his throat and bit down hard. He was bleeding, and all she had to do was hold on, ignite her fire, and The Darkness would be dead.

Dead.

Dead like her.

Kane would be dead. Her heart shattered.

Everything had gotten so messed up. With a heartbroken bellow, she released his neck and backed off him. She waited for the fire. She waited for the teeth and claws, but The Darkness just lay there, his head held high, throat bleeding red on black scales. A soft hum was coming from him. It was the same comforting sound she used to make to Harper when they were kids. When she and Wyatt were in a fight and Harper's dragon needed comfort.

The sound became louder, more prehistoric, rattling at different frequencies. The rage in Rowan's veins evaporated and was replaced by the weight of what had happened.

Her time with Kane was cut to nothing. There would be no happy life, no more feeling safe. With a bellow, Rowan shrank into her human form and fell forward onto her knees, covered her face with her hands, and screamed as long and as loud as she could.

The Darkness could kill her if he wanted. She was already dead anyway.

He didn't, though. Instead, he curled his body around her, limping on his missing back leg. Long neck, long body, wings tucked against his back, long tail, he encircled her and let off the comforting sound again as she fell apart in the middle of the destroyed, burning forest.

She could hear sirens now, loud and blaring. The Darkness would kill anyone who threatened him, and she couldn't risk civilian casualties.

"Kane," she sobbed. "If you're in there, Change back."

The Darkness growled a terrifying sound, but she stood and strode to him, pressed her hands to his face. His spikes pierced her palms, and she winced away. His eye was the size of her face, and his pupil dilated and constricted as he focused on her.

"Please, Kane. You've already hurt me. Don't hurt anyone else."

His eye softened and seemed to study her for a few moments before The Darkness's form blurred and shrank until all that remained was the man. Kane knelt by a felled tree, weight resting on his clenched fists and his knees. His ribs were badly burned, and red trickled from his neck. Smoke drifted all around them, carried by the wind.

The sirens were loud now, close. Blue and red lights flashed through the smog, and then black hummers surrounded them.

She wouldn't ever see Kane again, and before he was taken away from her, he needed to understand what he'd done. "You burned my treasure."

"Hands in the air, both of you!" an officer yelled. The crack of weapons being cocked was deafening.

"I didn't, Rowan," Kane said, placing his hands behind his head. "I didn't burn your treasure."

"I watched you!" she screamed.

Kane gritted his teeth and shook his head, eyes trained on her, his hair covering half of his fearsome face. "What does it feel like, Roe? Do you feel loss? Do you feel lost? That wasn't your treasure!"

"Hands on your head!" an officer said from behind her.

Rowan linked her hands behind her head. "You killed me."

"I didn't, baby. I didn't. I was there. I was in control."

"Oh yeah? When you burned 1010?"

"No, after, when you Changed. I was there, Roe. I was there!"

"You burned the fucking mountains!" she screamed.

One of the officers, dressed in black gear,

jammed a needle into Kane's neck. The officers were taking him away now toward one of the black Hummers. "I was there, Roe, tell them. Don't let them take me to Apex." He was shoved in the back, and right before the door closed beside him, Kane yelled, "Don't let them take him from me again!"

And as the Hummer picked its way through the shattered forest and disappeared from her view, warmth trickled out of her nose and splatted against the dry leaves at her feet.

Rowan wiped her nose on her bare shoulder, and red smeared across her pale skin.

And so The Sickening began.

TWENTY-ONE

A week in this place, and Kane was already going mad. He paced the length of the room, then back to the door and slammed his palm onto it. He had to get back to Rowan. He had to save her because right now she would be sickening without him.

Kane pounded on the door again and was startled when it lurched open. It was Dr. Mir.

"Again?" Kane asked.

"Yep." A short, squat doctor with a clipboard in one hand and a Taser in the other, he was dressed in fireproof gear, like always.

This wasn't like the first time Kane had gone through Apex. Other than the first dose of meds to subdue the dragon, Kane hadn't been given anything in seven days.

Seven days away from his mate, and he wouldn't be able to hold back The Darkness much longer.

He grabbed the cane by the door and leaned heavily on it as he walked out. "Has she called?" he asked as Dr. Mir followed him down the cement hallway. "Or sent a letter? Anything?"

"Easy Kane. I told you, if she tries for contact, we won't keep you apart."

His voice sounded truthful when he said that. Huh. Apex had gone and gotten a soul in the years he'd been away from the program.

Dr. Mir guided him to a cavernous space he called the Changing Room. The walls were made of rock, and electric currents flashed like laser beams around the outer edge. On part of the wall was two-way mirror glass, so scientists could study his shifts and pick him apart. As far as he could tell, Kane had been taken to some deep cave system. Likely very few in the world knew where he was. He could escape, though. He had the power to, but Dr. Mir kept promising if he played nice, good things would happen. And Kane hoped to God those good things were visitations with Rowan.

If she ever wanted to talk to him again.

Kane stood in the center of a large painted X in the middle of the room and waited for Dr. Mir to get into place behind the fireproof screen and give him the signal.

Dr. Mir flicked his fingers. Kane inhaled deeply, closed his eyes, and let The Darkness rip out of his body. Only it wasn't like before when he was a boy. Thoughts of Rowan anchored him to his dragon, and he was there, fully present, driving the animal. The room wasn't big enough and didn't leave much space to move around. Uncomfortably, Kane circled, limping on the bad leg. There was no room above to stretch his wings, and they were sore from being tucked up for too long.

"Head to the right," Dr. Mir said in a bored voice.

Okay. Kane turned his head to the right.

"Now left."

Kane did it and sighed a breath that dislodged a healthy layer of dirt off the cement floor.

"Am I boring you, Kane?" Dr. Mir asked in an amused tone.

Kind of. He just wanted to see Rowan. Nothing else. He just wanted to see her again.

"Change back."

This part sucked. They didn't let him stay in dragon form too long, and the quick Changes hurt his body. They left his muscles feeling pulled, fatigued, and aching down to his bones for hours afterward.

Kane tucked The Darkness away and stood there panting, sweating, balancing on his good leg.

Dr. Mir brought him his cane and grinned. "You have a visitor."

The pain evaporated in an instant. "Is it her?"

"This way," Dr. Mir clipped out, leaving Kane to hobble behind the doctor toward the door they came in.

Kane was led down a hallway he'd never been down before. It was lengthy, and his steps echoed for a long time. Kane narrowed his eyes at the back of Dr. Mir's head. If this was the part where they put him down, Kane was going to burn this fucking facility to the ground.

He didn't have much fear anymore.

Dr. Mir opened a door on the right and waited for Kane to enter. Kane paused at the sight of the man sitting in the center of the room at a metal table. He knew him. Didn't mean he wanted to be in the same room as him.

"Go on," Dr. Mir said.

Kane scanned the room for possible escapes. The door behind him was the only exit, but there was two-way glass in here, too. If things got hairy, he could smash through that and find an escape through there.

"Kane, sit," the man said. "Please."

He wore a dark suit, and his dark hair was streaked gray at the temples. His silver eyes tightened at the corners, and his pupils elongated.

"Damon," Kane greeted him somberly. He pulled out a metal chair and sat down across the table from the blue dragon himself. From the man he'd feared all his life.

"You've done well in here," Damon said. "Better than I expected."

Kane frowned and cast a glance up at the camera in the corner. Leaning forward, he clasped his hands and asked, "What do you mean?"

"This is my facility, Kane."

"You own Apex?" he asked through the raging hum of his dragon.

"This isn't Apex. This place isn't designed to strip

away animals, Kane. It's designed to rehabilitate them."

Shocked, Kane leaned back in his chair. "How...but the police arrested me."

"My people got to you first. I had them on the ground, waiting for Rowan to make her decision."

"Make her decision," Kane repeated low.

"To bite you and release your dragon. Wouldn't have worked if she didn't love you, Kane. It wouldn't have worked if her dragon didn't choose yours. If she didn't call your animal from you. We knew it would be bad. Knew it would be rough when your dragon emerged because he'd been locked inside of you for so long, but Rowan..."

"Kicked my ass?"

Damon chuckled low, and his eyes lost some of their tightness. "You let her. You were trying not to hurt her."

"How do you know?"

"Your epic dragon battle was videotaped from three different angles from three different bystanders in the Smoky Mountains. She was tempted to kill you for burning the cabin, and you were going to let her."

"The cabin was collateral damage."

"Ah," Damon said, nodding once. "You managed to do something I've been trying to do for years."

"And what's that?"

Damon's mouth set in a grim line. "Prove to Rowan that sheet of warped metal wasn't her treasure. She clung too damn tight to it. She's stubborn like me, and like her father. Once she picks something, she picks it."

"Were you responsible for her luggage getting lost on the plane?" he asked.

Damon gave a slight smile and nodded.

"Were you responsible for her sitting next to me on the plane?"

Another nod. "All I could do was put her in your path though, Kane. You had to rise up and do the rest."

"I didn't rise, sir. Rowan did. Your girl is a beautiful destroyer."

"Just like I always knew she could be. She needed you to show her that, though." Damon pushed a few buttons on his phone and shoved it across the table to Kane.

A video played.

News stories showed a battle between a

Blackwing Dragon and a smaller, gray-scaled Bloodrunner Dragon. Him blowing fire on the mountains and burning the cabin. The battle on the ground after they'd tumbled to earth. And then it cut to videos of Rowan speaking in front of crowds with the Bloodrunners standing behind her.

"Kane's a good man, in control of his dragon, and the battle was a direct result of what Apex Genetic Testing does to shifters. I demand that the hunt for him be called off, and that Apex be shut down immediately. This is a matter of shifter rights. They have been stripped from my mate, and I want him back." Rowan looked the camera dead on. "I need him back."

And then there was home video of Rowan standing over a sink, Harper holding her hair back as blood streamed from Rowan's mouth and nose.

"It's okay, Roe, we'll get him back," Harper murmured. "Beck, what do we do? Should we take her to him? It's getting really bad." Harper turned a panicked look to a woman in a dark gray business suit standing behind them.

"If she stops the tour now, Kane won't be safe out of hiding. He won't be safe outside of Damon's facility. If we don't take the heat off him, the government and Apex will be after him the second he steps out of hiding. Rowan, you'll always be on the run, and your mate will always be at risk."

"I can do this," Rowan said, steel in her voice. Blood gushed, and she retched. Harper rubbed her back, but the Bloodrunner alpha looked scared.

Beck held Rowan's phone in front of her. "See if this helps."

On the screen was a picture Rowan had taken of them. In it, she was kissing his cheek and looked radiant with happiness, and Kane was even smiling.

"It doesn't work anymore," Rowan murmured in a weak voice. "I need to hold him. I need to see him. I need the fucking charges to be lifted."

"Ryder." Harper looked at the person behind the camera. "Go get some towels. Stop hugging Kane's prosthetic leg. He's in hiding, not dead. And shut that damn camera off. No one needs to see this. If I find it on your social media, I'm gonna burn your ass."

The video went shaky, and then faded to black.

"Fuck," Kane murmured, grimacing away from the phone. "Let me go to her, please Damon. I can fix her. I can make her feel better. I can stop The

Sickening. I'm her treasure. I know I am. It's my dragon. It was always the dragon. Just...let me see her."

"Since no one was hurt and since the Bloodrunners, the Ashe Crew, the Gray Backs, the Boarlanders, the Winterset Coven, and Ben Porter's Red Havoc Crew have been tirelessly rallying for you, it was announced today that all charges have been dropped. I've submitted video of your controlled Changes to law enforcement, and they have called off the search for you. This morning it was announced that you are free. You will always be listed as a dangerous shifter, Kane. That's something no one can fix, and you'll have to be careful every day. There won't be second chances—not for a shifter like you. But if you work hard enough, you can still have a good life. With Rowan."

Kane dragged in a shaky breath as relief flooded his body. All the shifters had rallied for him with his brave Rowan at the head of it all. He'd never cried before, but damn if his eyes didn't burn right now.

Damon stood and nodded his head toward the exit. Kane rose and leaned heavily on his cane as he followed the old dragon out into the hallway and then through a maze that led them eventually to an elevator.

Damon Daye stood straight-backed and proud, his hands clasped in front of his lap as the elevator took them up. And right before they reached the sunlight, Damon turned and clasped Kane's hand. "Thank you for what you've done for my girl. You take care of each other. Always. And if you ever need anything, call me. You remind me…" Damon cleared his throat and dropped Kane's hand. "You remind me of all the good parts of your father. The parts I've missed."

Sunlight hit Kane in the face, and he squinted, shielded his face with his hand, and when his eyes adjusted, he could see Damon walking away toward a black Town Car.

The man opened the back door, and the most beautiful sight Kane had ever seen stepped out.

Rowan was wearing a pink sundress and flip flops, and her blond hair was whipping around her shoulders. She was already crying as she ran for him. Kane rushed, leaning on his cane harder and harder. He was ready when Rowan leapt through the air and wrapped herself around him. She buried her face against his neck, her body racked with sobs. And fuck, he never wanted to stop holding her. He pulled her in tight against him, looked up at the blue sky, and tried to remember how to breathe.

"I'm sorry," he chanted over and over.

"It's okay. I thought you were burning my treasure. I thought you were trying to hurt me, but you weren't. I love you, Kane, I love you." Rowan eased back and cupped his beard. He probably looked like shit right now—tired, unshaven, and still healing from the burns she'd given him—but Rowan was staring at him as if she'd never seen anything so stunning.

Kane cupped the back of her head and kissed her. Rowan slid down, stood on her own two feet, and slipped her arms around his shoulders. The damn tension in his chest eased with every moment that he touched her lips with his.

Rowan disengaged and rubbed her soft cheek against his. "Kane, you knew all along, didn't you?" she whispered.

"Knew what, dragon?" There was no more calling her princess because she'd gone fearlessly to war with The Darkness and won.

Her breath hitched, and a smile stretched her face. Slowly she leaned forward until her lips were right by his ear. And then she whispered something that banished every hurt he'd ever endured.

"You aren't Dark Kane anymore. You're *my* Kane." She leaned up on her tiptoes and kissed him gently. "You're my treasure."

EPILOGUE

Kane was laughing that easy sound Rowan had fallen in love with as he gave her a piggy-back ride around the house to the front porch. He was dragging a pair of two-by-fours in one arm and dropped them with a clatter in the front yard.

"Today is the big day," she murmured excitedly as she climbed down to the ground.

"Mmm," he rumbled, his soft brown eyes dancing. He was shirtless and sweaty from working, but she didn't mind him hugging her. "What day is that?"

"The day we finish our home. It's a big deal."

"So you're sure you aren't going to disappear on me and go back to Damon's Mountains?"

Rowan clamped her teeth over the claiming mark she'd given him. "Sorry, Blackwing, you're stuck with me."

Kane licked his bottom lip and hugged her closer, opened his mouth to say something, but the hum of approaching engines sounded through the valley.

With a dangerous look, he narrowed his eyes on the road. He didn't stoop down and pull his knife from his ankle on reflex anymore. Now he trusted The Darkness to protect them from whatever came their way.

When the pair of trucks pulled to a stop in his front yard, Kane relaxed and gave Weston a two fingered wave. The Bloodrunners piled out and greeted them. Ryder picked Kane up in a back-cracking hug while Alana hugged Rowan.

"What are you guys doing here?" Kane asked. In the last six months, the Bloodrunners had only come here a few times. Rowan was pretty sure it was because Kane's dragon felt huge and terrifying, and they were trying to give him space to lay claim to his territory.

Ryder held up a case of canned margaritas. "We're here to celebrate, naturally."

"Celebrate the house being done?" Kane asked, confusion knitting his dark eyebrows into a frown.

Weston lowered the tailgate of his truck and pulled out a couple of cheap plastic forest green shutters and a wooden board.

Kane's face fell, and his cheeks tinged with shame. He ran his hand up the back of his head and ducked his gaze. "Are those from ten-ten?"

"Yeah, we saved a few bits and pieces of her. Figured you could use some of the mojo on your place."

"You aren't pissed that I destroyed it?" Kane asked quietly.

Lexi held up a plastic cage with a little black and white mouse with giant testicles. Sammy Scrotum, mascot of the old cabin. "The important parts survived."

Weston dropped the shutters on the ground and handed Kane the large, misshapen wooden cut-out. It was charred around the edges but there were four numbers still nailed crookedly to it. *1010*.

Rowan put her hands over her mouth to cover her emotions. She'd been heartbroken over the loss of 1010, but it wasn't lost at all. It was just moving.

Avery rested her head on Rowan's shoulder. Already, Rowan's vision was blurred with tears, and she still had work to do.

Kane swallowed hard as he took the plank of wood from Weston's grasp. With a crooked smile, Kane hopped up on the porch, picked up the hammer and a couple of nails, and secured the plaque to his cabin.

The gurgling of a baby sounded, and Rowan smiled as Harper approached with baby Hudson in her arms. Wyatt walked beside his mate, a proud smile on his boy. Harper had been strong enough. She'd survived having her baby Bloodrunner boy, and now she looked so beautiful. Hair down in waves, her eyes so full of emotion already as she came to a stop right in front of Kane.

"Blackwing Dragon," Harper said formally. "I've thought about this so much. Thought about your place here, right next to my mountains. I've thought about how lonely it must've been for you walking through life with no crew. You feel like a part of us." She swallowed hard. "After Hudson was born and when I got my dragon back, I had planned on asking you to be a part of my crew, but after talking to

Rowan, I don't think that would be fair to you. Your dragon is too big, too dominant, and it's too much for one crew."

"It's okay," Kane murmured, pressing his finger against Hudson's searching hand. Rowan didn't miss the sadness in his voice, though.

"I can offer you friendship and a steady ally if you ever need us," Harper said.

"I understand," he whispered thickly, his eyes on baby Hudson.

"Kane?" Rowan said, pulling the folded paperwork out of her back pocket. "Here."

With a confused frown, Kane studied her face, then looked at the others before he took the papers and unfolded them. Aloud he read, "Blackwing Crew. Application for Second in the crew. Rowan Barnett." Kane inhaled sharply, and now his eyes were full of emotion as he rubbed his chin. "Are these crew registration papers?"

Rowan nodded. "Say the word, and I'll turn these in. We'll start from scratch, me and you. Say the word, and I won't be a Gray Back anymore, Kane. I'll be a Blackwing." She turned her face and exposed her neck to him. With an emotional laugh at his shocked face, she murmured, "Alpha."

Kane turned his back, covered his face with his palms, his body rigid as the papers fluttered in his hands. She scented the air, but he didn't smell angry. Suddenly, Kane rounded on her and lifted her off the ground, hugged her tightly against his chest. "You gonna be my crew, Roe?"

She petted the back of his head, over the scars Apex left on him, and smiled at the Boodrunners behind them. "Yeah, Kane. I'll be your crew."

He had told her once that if he ever got The Darkness back, if would be the end of him. But it wasn't.

It was the beginning of Kane's Mountains.

BLACKWING DRAGON

Want more of these characters?

Blackwing Dragon is the fifth book in a five book series based in Harper's Mountains.

Check out these other books from T. S. Joyce.

Bloodrunner Dragon
(Harper's Mountains, Book 1)

Bloodrunner Bear
(Harper's Mountains, Book 2)

Air Ryder
(Harper's Mountains, Book 3)

Novak Raven
(Harper's Mountains, Book 4)